Ghost Engine

Also by Christian TeBordo

Toughlahoma
The Awful Possibilities
We Go Liquid
Better Ways of Being Dead
The Conviction and Subsequent Life of Savior Neck

CHRISTIAN TeBORDO

GHOST ENGINE

STORIES

BRIDGE EIGHT PRESS | JACKSONVILLE, FLORIDA

The stories in this collection were previously published in the following publications: "The Star Thrower-Thrower," in *Always Crashing*; "A Modest Book Proposal from Pete Maynard, Author of *M__y Dick*," in *The Collagist*; "Bear Country," in *Hobart*; "One to No One," in *Juked*; "The American Family Robinson," in *Bridge Eight Literary Magazine*; "How We Lived on Main Street," in *Vol. 1 Brooklyn*'s Sunday Stories; "Smaller Still" (as "How We Keep it Fresh), in *PANK*; "Whose Bridesmaid?," in *Sententia*; "This House Is Not a Mansion, and God Is Not a Ghost" (as "For Faithless Wives, on the Nightly Removel of Prosthetic Limbs"), in *A Book of Uncommon Prayer* (Outpost 19 Books).

Published by Bridge Eight Press
Jacksonville, Florida

www.bridgeeight.com

ISBN 978-1-7323667-3-2
E-ISBN 978-1-7323667-4-9
LCCN 2019940287

Printed in the USA
Distributed by Small Press Distribution
Cover & book design by Jared Rypkema

for Timothy, Fragonard to my Watteau

The term et al. was made for me. But I can't remember how.
– Barry Hannah, "Nicodemus Bluff"

Don't you want to have a body?
– One chatbot to another

Organs

Ghost Engine

The Star Thrower-Thrower

FRAG AND WATT HAVE WORKED ALL MORNING ON THE GHOST ENGINE.
Neither of them is mechanically trained or inclined, but here is the wrench and here the rag, and between them they've got the bolts tightened, the surfaces sparkling. After several hours' tweaking and buffing, the Ghost Engine finally looks like an engine. It looks exactly like a ghost engine.

And yet, when Frag switches the switch from off to on, the only result is the sound of the switch switching. Frag switches the switch from on to off, back to on, off again, faster and faster as frustration mounts. The sound, at this speed, of the switch's switching, is something like the click of an engine, but a small, simple engine, nothing so grand as you'd expect from a machine as magnificent as the Ghost Engine. And supposing, Watt thinks—Watt is free to think as he sits beside the engine, rag in hand, watching as Frag switches and switches, sweat beginning to bead at Frag's hairline and around his upper lip—again, supposing, Watt thinks, that this rapid clicking were the true and appropriate sound of a functioning Ghost Engine, that still wouldn't suggest that the engine was functioning properly as an engine. It requires altogether too much effort from its operator to be worthy of the name engine, much less Ghost Engine.

The engine's operator, that is, Frag, no longer looks frustrated. He's angry now, shirtless, face a wet red. There is a scent of hot metal in the air around the engine. Look at Frag, a moving portrait of impotent rage, Watts thinks, but too late; Frag already has the wrench in the air above his head, and the wrench is not small.

Down it comes, and up again and down, battering Watt about the shoulders like a pain engine. This is not, thinks Watt ... but the word won't come. His last thought, as consciousness fades, is: relatable. This is not relatable. But can that be right?

Watt comes to, finds Frag seated beside him, elbows on knees, using his shirt like a towel to wipe the slick from his skin as he stares at the horizon. He hasn't noticed Watt's waking. The wrench is on the ground between them. Watt reaches out, grips the handle, slides it toward himself slowly, silently. Frag rests forehead on forearms, spent. Watt rolls onto his side, conceals the wrench behind his back.

"Frag," he says, "what do you think they mean by 'relatability?'"

Frag raises his head but doesn't turn.

"They?" he asks.

"The kids," says Watt. "The children."

"The youth, you mean. Easy. The youth want to watch Hermione Granger order a cup of coffee in the Starbucks language."

"Hermione Granger?"

"From Harry Potter. They want to watch her place the order with the girl at the register while, in her head, she tries out the word *barista... barista* in a variety of accents, never settling on a single pronunciation, never working up the courage to say the word aloud," Frag says. "They want the barista to understand exactly what Hermione means when she orders in the Starbucks language, and to know how to spell the name *Hermione* with a grease pencil on an empty paper cup. They'll want to watch Hermione move to the other end of the counter where she'll unlock her phone and look up the pronunciation of *barista*, but, unable to decipher the phonetic symbols, will shortly swipe her thumb across the screen and scroll through still photos depicting the magical adventures she's had with her friends. These photos will produce in her a melancholic nostalgia, a nostalgic melancholy. It's been so long since she's had an adventure! But then she'll remind herself that those adventures were trying; she didn't exactly enjoy adventuring while adventuring. She prefers having adventured to adventuring, prefers it by a long shot. In fact, this nostalgic melancholy, or melancholic nostalgia, is the closest thing to actual happiness she's ever felt. And besides, isn't ordering coffee in the Starbucks language and then receiving the exact coffee that you ordered a kind of adventure in itself? At the precise moment this thought occurs to her, the youth want another barista to call out her name —"

"Hermione Granger."

"No," says Frag, "Just Hermione. Recall she didn't give the girl at the register her full name. The youth expect the girl at the pick-up counter to say, simply, 'Hermione,' and then to hand Hermione her coffee, which Hermione will accept, also with a smile. I guaran-goddamn-tee you that, at that moment, the youth will smile as well. And sigh."

Watt doesn't follow.

"She'll drink the coffee, of course," Frag tells him. "The youth will want it to be hot in the hand but to land lukewarm on the tongue. They'll want her to have the sense of acute focus that they think they get from coffee, but not the dirty jitters and pungent sweats that come at the bottom of the cup, to say nothing of the crankiness, the eventual weight gain that, outside the world of relatability, comes from consuming the heaping piles of processed sugars and artificial sweeteners that they wanted Hermione to request in the Starbucks language in order to disguise the bitter flavor of actual coffee, which is all the more bitter when it comes from Starbucks. But in the Starbucks of the relatable, everything is as you'd want it."

"I'm not sure this example is quite illuminating," says Watt.

"No single example is going to illuminate any phenomenon worth examining. So consider Wolverine."

"The mutant."

"That word sounds so filthy coming from your mouth," says Frag. "Say it again."

"Mutant," says Watt.

"*Mutant*," says Frag. "I love it. Wolverine the *mutant*. Canadian-born super-soldier-cum-vigilante anti-hero. Bad attitude. Bone-blades in the backs of his hands. Adamantium skeleton. Ability to heal his own injuries almost instantaneously."

"Canadian?" says Watt. "I recall, from my own youth, an Australian accent."

"Non-canonical," Frag says. "What is canon is that he is more than a century old now, and it's time to put his brawling days behind him. The youth would like to see him choose vegetarianism.

They want him to choose veganism and *stick with it* this time!"

"That won't save any animals," says Watt, "or improve his health. Wolverine's a fiction. He doesn't exist."

"Do not inform the youth," says Frag.

"And if he did exist," Watt says, "how could the youth relate to his hanging up the superhero leotards at the age of one hundred forty?"

"It's the veganism, and the struggle with veganism, that they wish to relate to. But if that doesn't help to clarify, take Garfield."

"What could the youth possibly want from Garfield?"

"The youth, my friend, desire Garfield and Odie to announce their pregnancy at last. They want weekly updates. 'At this point, your fetus is the size of a .22 calibre bullet.' 'By now, your fetus's tale is shaped like a cartoon heart.' 'Toward the end of this trimester, your child will be capable of trimming its own mustache in the womb.' The youth emphatically do *not* want to be present for the labor and delivery, but they do, all of them, wish to watch the happy couple tend the tray of lasagna that Garfield will give birth to, lovingly, for all of eternity. *That* lasagna will never be consumed."

"I think I'm starting to understand," Watt says, "but I doubt I'll ever relate."

"It's just another engine," says Frag, "a static engine."

"Like our Ghost Engine," says Watt.

"Wrong," Frag says. "The Ghost Engine is not meant to be static; it's simply broken. The relatable engine is functioning exactly as it's supposed to. It gives the appearance of dynamism by turning in on itself when confronted with a more complex phenomenon. It's built to deny that anything can happen, to give the illusion that what it's already doing constitutes the only possible action."

"Like in the story of the starfish," says Watt.

"I don't know any starfish stories," Frag says.

Watt reaches subtly behind himself, pats around to confirm that the wrench is where he left it, leaves his hand on the handle.

"Everyone knows this story," he says. "An old man and a little boy, his grandson probably, are walking along the beach, and they stumble on thousands of starfish, scattered and piled over the shore — left behind, I guess, by retreating tides."

"I think maybe I *have* heard it after all," says Frag.

"The kid runs up to the starfish and starts throwing them into the water, eagerly if not frantically. He gets winded after a while, and the grandpa says, 'Give it up! There's thousands of 'em. You're never gonna make a difference.' The kid looks down at the starfish in his hand, tosses it into the ocean, smiles, and says, wisely, 'I made a difference to that one.'"

"Nope," says Frag. "Never heard it. The story I know concerns a sage old grandpa and a cynical brat."

"There are different versions," Watt says. "They can be arranged to flatter the teller or the listener, depending on who needs flattering."

"When you told the one about the kid just now, I wanted to throw the kid himself into the ocean, possibly hold him under a while. I think you threw that 'wisely' in there specifically to stoke my rage."

Only now does Watt realize how tightly he's gripping the wrench. His palm is damp and his knuckles ache.

"I intentionally told it in a way that flatters neither of us," he says, "to show that the way the story is told misses the larger point."

"Which is?" says Frag.

"What difference does it make?"

"To the starfish or the kid?"

"What difference could anything make to a starfish? A starfish is unequipped to understand or to sense difference," Watt says. "Starfish have neither head nor heart."

"So the only difference is that the kid thinks he made a difference," says Frag.

"Not much of a difference at all, is it?"

Frag is staring at him now. Watt doesn't recall exactly when Frag turned his way, can only hope Frag can't see what Watt is doing behind his back. What he's doing is stretching his fingers, trying to shake some feeling back into his hand.

"You sound like the cynical grandpa," Frag says. "'You'll never make a difference because there's no difference to make.'"

"But there's *only* difference to make," says Watt. "Difference is a people thing, and only people are capable of gaining anything from parables. So how could the parable be about making a difference for people?"

"If the *starfish* were people…"

Watt can practically see the real point of the starfish story washing over Frag's face, gentle as a low tide. Frag is beautiful, he thinks. Frag is his friend. For a moment Watt has the feeling that, together, they could actually make this Ghost Engine work, if they could just stop beating each other with the only tools they have. But there isn't much chance of that. He wipes his wet hand against the seat of his pants and grabs the wrench stranglingly as Frag says:

"Why the fuck are all these bodies washing up on the shore!"

The Wrong Mother

MOM, THEY'RE SHOUTING, HEY MOM, LIKE IT'S AN EMERGENCY, WHICH IT always sounds like an emergency with these two, Come quick, and I do, I go so fast I'm at the backdoor with it swinging out and away toward the siding before they can say anything else in case they're not the boys who cried wolf this time, but it's not an emergency, it's a mess, a mess all over the backyard with my old exercise bike at its center, the Bad One on its seat hunched forward with his hands on the handlebars, legs dangling down, the Worse One kneeling beside the bike like he's trying to measure the distance between his brother's feet and the pedals, which is considerable, the distance, and I'm thinking, these two so-called prodigies can't figure out the way to get the gears turning is to slip off the seat and stand on the pedals, but there's no way I'm telling them because I'm also thinking, This is only half the mess, that bike having come from the garage, and not just the garage, but deep in the garage, surrounded by endless walls and stacks of junk, way more junk than is out here on the lawn, which means the garage is a disaster area too, and I tell them, You boys have got a lot of picking up to do before dinnertime, and they say, Forget it Mom, when our new startup gets off the ground we'll be able to pay some poor bastard from the neighborhood to clean up after us, so why don't you go call the news tipline and tell them we invented a brand-new, boy-powered flying machine, and now they mention it I can see there's a method to their mess, like they got an open golf umbrella sticking up from the back frame, and there's a pair of mismatched kites sticking off each side must be meant for wings, but one thing I am *not* gonna do is call the tipline, bring them out to make some heartwarming human interest story about a couple of cute, dim-witted boys pedaling like crazy at a stationary bike, if they ever even figure out how to pedal it, all the time imagining they're flying, because even if they make them look sweet and wide-eyed, which would be deception itself, half the neighbors would sit there watching while they eat their dinners thinking, What a couple of stupids, making a mess of their poor mom's backyard thinking they've made some major contribution to the repository of human knowledge when they're really just wasting everyone's time, but I don't tell them that, and I don't tell them I'm not gonna call the news, I just go back into the kitchen to finish making dinner, let them think what they want, and that's what they do, I know because I've just got the table set and am about ready to call them in for dinner when I hear them shouting, Mom, hey Mom, again and as usual like it's an emergency, but before I reach the door they're hollering, When's the newspeople coming? and I'm hollering back, The newspeople ain't, but I kind of trail off because I've got the door open now and I can see they ain't in the backyard, but I can still hear their voices shouting, Mom, Mom, when's the newspeople gonna get here, and it takes me a minute to realize their voices are coming from above, and for a second I'm scared to look but then I do, first just my eyes, then chin up, head back, and there they are, they figured out how to pedal, the Bad One standing astraddle the safety bar like I would have told him, the Worse One on the seat behind him, arms around his brother's shoulders, the umbrella spinning like some kind of chopper blade, kites flapping in the breeze, a piece of rope tied to the frame of the bike, stretched taut so I can follow it all the way to the ground where they've got it twisted and knotted through a pile of cinderblocks that I have no idea where they found, anchoring them, which is why the boys are flying in a wide circle over the property, not really going anywhere, and I yell up, You boys come down right now, and they yell down, We're staying up here til the newspeople come get their footage, so I suppose I got no choice but to go back inside and actually call the tipline this time, which I do, and when the voice on the other end says, Whaddaya got for me, I say, My boys developed some kind of flying machine and now they're zooming around over my backyard, and the voice says, How old you say these boys were? And I say, I didn't, but they're eight, both of them, twins, which is hell, don't try it, and he says, Lady that sounds dangerous, and I say, Having twins? tell me about it, and he says, No, lady, eight-year-old boys with their own flying machine, he says, We couldn't cover something like that, produce a segment on flying eight-year-olds, suddenly every eight-year-old in town is trying out their own flying machines, breaking necks, damaging *property*, probably the seven- and nine-year-olds too, and that'd be on us, but maybe if they were just, you know, on the ground with a little propeller spinning, just, you know, imagining they were flying, maybe that'd be, not newsworthy, but heartwarming and human interestful, but flying? actually flying? no way lady, you've got to get them down, and I tell him, My boys won't come down until the newspeople show up and they're stubborn, my boys, and he says, Well that's between you and them, that ain't on me, and hangs up, and I go out to the backyard and say, News ain't coming, but the boys ain't where they were before, much higher now, must have let out a bunch of rope, and I wonder where they got that rope and how much of it they got, which gives me an idea, so I yell up, How much more rope you got up there, and they yell down, This is all we got, and I say, So you can't get up any higher? and they say, Not so long as we're anchored, and I'm thinking, so long as they're attached to the rope and that's all the rope there is, my plan, which is to pull the rope from the bottom, arm over arm, until my boys are back on solid ground, my plan, that is, might work, but the boys seem to be on to me because before I even get my fists around a length of rope they're yelling down, Hey Mom, more like for attention than an emergency, and when I look up they don't have to say anything because the Worse One is brandishing my gardening shears like the villain in a silent movie to let me know if I try to bring them down they'll go up and up instead, all the way to the moon maybe, so I'll never see them again, which doesn't sound so bad but I'm their mom, so I back away from the rope with my hands in the air like peace, like please don't shoot, and say again, News ain't coming, and they say, You didn't even call, and I say, Yes I did, they said it was too dangerous, and the boys say, All of them? you called every news station? because it doesn't seem like you were in there long enough to call every news station, like maybe you were in there long enough to call just one, but not long enough to have used your full powers of persuasion, and before I can start recounting the whole conversation like the responsibility's mine, the smoke detector's going off, which means dinner's already ruined, and now I have a choice to make, either stay outside trying to convince the boys to come down, or go put out the fire, risk chopper crash or inferno, and when it comes down to it, I can only really be blamed for one of them, so I go back in and the kitchen is a cloud of thick black smoke so I feel my way to the stove and turn the knob then run around opening all the windows and waving my hands in front of my face like swatting flies and when the smoke finally clears it turns out I was right, dinner is ruined, but the house is saved and the boys must still be up in the air because I can hear them doing that fake coughing for attention that boys sometimes do, and one of them hollers, Jeez, what are you trying to do, Mom, smoke us out, which doesn't make sense because they're not even in, which is the problem, so I know the only other thing to do is call the other tiplines and try to use my powers of persuasion, but there's no persuading the next two tiplines, too dangerous, too dangerous, that'd be on us, maybe if it was just a couple of boys imagining they were flying, and it's dusk now, which makes me wonder how long they can keep it up, they've been quiet for a while, maybe they've come down after all, so I go and check, and nope, they're still up there and somehow they've switched places, the Bad One on the seat, the Worse One pedaling, and it seems like they've got nothing to say to me, like they already know I've got nothing to say to them, and soon it'll be full dark, not the time to point news cameras at the sky, and there's only one tipline left, but I've got one last idea when I remember what all the other tiplines said, maybe if it was just two boys *imagining* they made a flying machine, so I call the last tipline and use my powers of persuasion, really lay it on thick, lie through my teeth, say, I've got these two, beautiful, wide-eyed boys, twins, and you will not *believe* what they're doing, they've been out in the backyard all day building what they think is a flying machine—exercise bike, umbrella, kites, the works—and now they're out there pedaling, and it's so cute because they're not even tall enough to reach the pedals from the seat, but they think they're flying, they're not imagining, they really believe they're up in the air, and it's just so goshdarn adorable and full of human interest that I think you better get a camera crew on out here right now, and the tipline guy says, You say they're eight years old? and I think maybe my powers of persuasion have actually worked, and I say, Yes, eight each, twins, don't try this at home, and the tipline guy says, Lady, first, two boys using their imaginations in the backyard is not a news story, and second, it's nine o'clock at night and those boys shouldn't be out in the backyard, they should be in bed, and then hangs up before I can tell him I know they should be in bed, that's exactly the problem, and anyway, they're not imagining or believing, they're *actually* flying, so the joke's on him, the joke's on all of us, but especially on me, because they're still up there and they aren't coming down even though the sky is black and the moon is new and they're singing, "Mom is so dumb, Mom is so dumb, we could have been the Wright brothers, instead we had the wrong mother," which means tomorrow morning, bright and early, I'm going to have to go on over to the WalMart and buy the biggest video camera they got, a trenchcoat, and a fedora, all on credit if it isn't already maxed out, and I'm going to have to hope that they're up there high enough that my newsman disguise fools them, at least long enough for me to get them down, but either way, it's just not fair, it's so unfair, I realized a long time ago that the twins were never gonna live in my reality, but what I don't know is why that means I should have to live in theirs

A Modest Book Proposal from Pete Maynard, Author of *M__y Dick*

DEAR EDITOR,

Congratulations on the success you've had with *Pride and Prejudice and Zombies!* I'm sure it's well-deserved, even though I haven't actually had the chance to read it yet. There's a waiting list for it at the local library and I don't need to tell you I'm a long way down, plus I can't afford to just go out and buy a copy.

Listen, this is what it's about right here and now.

I hope you aren't currently working on a monster mashup of a certain classic about a big white whale. Or actually it's neither here nor there if you are as long as you still have room on your publishing schedule for what I'm proposing here which has nothing to do with *Moby Dick*. I'm just trying to give you some background if you'll bear with me.

Maybe you've heard of *M__y Dick*? I would bet you haven't read it, and I bet I'd win that bet because I'd be leaving nothing up to chance. Here's why: nobody has read *M__y Dick*. Scratch that. Nobody but me has read *M__y Dick*, because there's only one copy in existence and it's right here in my apartment, right here on this very desk I am writing to you from, in fact. That was the whole point. *M__y Dick* was just for me, for my own self-improvement. Of course, that didn't stop them from talking about it, which was fine at first, and then it was not.

But maybe I'm not making myself clear? It happens. It happens more than I'd like. Let me try harder, okay?

Back when I still had the job, I was not just resting on my laurels like some people or trying to get ahead by making my coworkers look bad like others. I was doing it the American way, with bootstraps and elbow grease and stick-to-itiveness. Self-improvement, I mean.

Like for instance, last year I did my vacation to Colonial Williamsburg instead of the beach or something. Did you know that in the 1700s they had a black guy there named Gowan something-or-other who was a Baptist preacher and not only was not a slave but even owned land? I didn't, not until that trip. I wondered if the other ones, the white ones and such, treated him with respect even though he was black, but could not think of how to say it. Either way I'm a better man for it. The vacation, I mean.

Then when fall came I thought that the theme of my self-improvement must be America, but there isn't much you can do about it when the weather gets cold, so I figured I might as well read a book. *The* book. The great American novel, which is *Moby Dick*.

A literary person like you has probably read *Moby Dick* about twenty times or how else would you know what would make a good monster mashup. Me, I had not read it before, and I did not really like it once I tried I'm sorry to admit. I like a good high seas adventure as much as the next red-blooded American male, but there did not seem to be much of that in the book, or maybe I was reading it wrong. Anyway, it did not seem to relate to me as a modern person, and I kept falling asleep trying to read it. It got to where I brought it to work, where I really could not just go to sleep, to read on my lunch break, but I still was almost nodding off every day and was about to finally give up when I got an idea.

One lunch, I was sitting at my desk with the book open but looking around asking myself if I shut the book would it also mean shutting the book on self-improvement and my eyes landed on my pen jar. The Sharpie in there stands out like a swollen swearfinger because it's so much thicker than all the pens and pencils, and I reached for it without really thinking. Sometimes I like to uncap it and see how long it takes the fumes to fill my cubicle, but this was not one of those times. This time I wanted to see how long it took me to blacken everything I'd read that day.

Not very long, it turned out. Maybe it was the idea of having something to do with my hands while I read, maybe it was the smell of the marker, but soon I wasn't just following the reading, I was absorbing it. And it was fun. Fun enough that I went back to the beginning, which was only thirty or so pages, and started from the start. Fun enough that I took the Sharpie and the book home with me and made it through another fifty pages. The next day I did ten more at lunch and seventy that night. I would have done more if I'd grabbed a whole handful of Sharpies, but I didn't get the idea to grab a whole handful until the first one crapped out on me in the middle of the second night.

Clarification: that first Sharpie crapped out on me in the middle of the second night, but I did not go and grab a handful of Sharpies from the office supply cabinet in the middle of the night. Those are two separate things!

Language: it's tricky. That was the whole point. Then and now.

So the third day I grabbed a whole handful of Sharpies from the supply cabinet, and after that I always had two or three with me to be prepared, which was a good thing because by then I was really plowing through that book. At the end of two weeks I had almost the whole thing read and blackened, less blackened than read, though, because a few days in I had hit on the idea of not blackening anything that was relevant to me as a modern person, which, let's be honest, was not much, but still.

The day came when I only had about fifteen pages left at the end of my lunch, and I decided to keep going to the end, and just as I got to the last page, somebody said, "*What* is that *smell?*"

I think it was Anne. Not the smell, but the person in the office who asked the question. I wasn't really paying attention because I was so close to the end.

Somebody else said: "Are you sniffing markers in there again, Maynard?"

That was Vick. I know for sure because I looked up as he stepped into my cube about three seconds later. He started coughing and waving his hands like he was going to die from Sharpie fume inhalation. I went back to *M__y Dick*.

"The fumes are a byproduct," I said, blackening another line.

"Of what?" said Vick.

"Of *M__y Dick*," I said.

"What the fuck are you trying to say?" said Vick.

When he said that I realized that what I'd said could be taken a certain way. I looked up to explain, but he'd seen what I was up to and was standing over me already.

"What's that?" he said, and grabbed the book from my hands. "*Moby Dick*?"

He started flipping through the book, first a page at a time and then a fan that blew his hair back a little, another gust of fumes to his face.

"It's all blacked out?" he said.

"No," I said, grabbing the book back, flipping it open to a particular page, and handing it to him.

"'My Dick?'" he read, "'Squeeze the sperm?'"

He tossed the book on my desk.

"There's something wrong with you," he said, and walked out.

I shrugged but there was no one left in my cube to shrug to. I went back to the book and blackened the last lines, but to tell the truth it was not as satisfying to finish as I thought it would be. I left it sitting on the edge of the desk and got back to work.

So what's the big deal? you're probably asking. Why is this guy wasting my extremely valuable time telling me about a book he doesn't even want me to publish which has nothing do with, and is really pretty much the opposite of, my specialty which is monster mashups?

A: I'm getting there as fast as I can! This is the exposition, and the climax of the exposition is that they got me. Vick must have told some of the other guys in the office about what happened, and one of the other guys complained to the boss that it was third party sexual harassment which I don't even know what that is. The boss didn't either, so he fired me for theft of company property when they noticed we were out of Sharpies.

Listen, I'm not going to pretend I think it's fair, but one of the things about self-improvement is that you can't dwell on the past. You've got to move forward without regrets and take no prisoners, so what I did was I found a lesson in all of it which is this:

There's two ways of doing things: addition and subtraction. Me, with my blacking out of *Moby Dick*, I was subtracting. You with your mashing up of *Pride and Prejudice and Zombies*, you were adding. That's why I'm broke and you're making money hand over fist.

Well I'm ready to add. I'm ready to make money hand over fist, so without further denouement, here is the big additional idea:

The Diary of Anne Frankenstein!

I probably don't need to explain to you that it will be the story of a smart, innocent young girl in hiding from the Nazis who gets the idea to create a monster, the original monster mashup, to wreak her vengeance upon them, but it backfires and the monster ends up hurting her and the people she loves. What you might not realize is that all it will take to make is a little cutting and pasting. Here is an example:

> According to the powers that be, I'm supposed to grin and bear it. But I can't! I have no intention of taking their insults lying down. I'll show them that Anne Frank wasn't born yesterday. They'll sit up and take notice and keep their big mouths shut when I make them see they ought to attend to their own manners instead of mine.

> It was with these feelings that I began the creation of a human being.

Now I know what you're thinking: You're thinking how do these two old stories have any relevance to us as modern human beings? Two things:

It's true that this is not exactly like what you did with *Pride and Prejudice and Zombies* by combining an old thing that is not relevant like *Pride and Prejudice*, which if you check their Wikipedia is actually about love, with something ultramodern that everybody cares and worries about such as zombies, and it's also true that all of the parts don't fit together as smoothly as the example I just showed you. A lot of the words of Frankenstein sound old-timey, while Anne Frank sounds pretty modern except less swearing. But the way around that is to use Babel Fish or something to translate the whole thing into Japanese and then back into English. Then we can have somebody turn it into a Manga by drawing Anne Frank sexier, with big eyes and whatnot. Then it would be even more of a mashup!

Listen, even if you don't know any Manga artists there is still thing number two:

Frankenstein is about resurrection, I think, and Anne Frank is about a girl and her family hiding from the Nazis. Like you didn't already know these things! The point is, they are not exactly on the cutting edge of the mind of every person you meet. But when you combine them, they are about revenge, which everyone is thinking about all of the time!

Okay, maybe not you. I know, you're not like everyone else. You live the life of the mind in an ivory tower made of gold that you earned from your fabulous success in the book biz. But what about everybody else? What about the little man? The guy sitting at home with nothing but a bunch of old library books that mean nothing to him because he got fired from his job over some pardononnez moi francais bullshit, and he can't afford to buy the modern ones which are all checked out of the library, and every second he feels like he might just go postal because he doesn't have the possibly illustrated story of someone like Anne Frankenstein and the monster she creates to just, you know, gorily disembowel her enemies with righteous fury, to keep him company and to identify with.

Going postal! What a fucking laugh. I told you I worked in a cubicle, and personally, I believe that living well is a dish best served cold. That's why I'm writing you today. Please consider giving me about a bathtub full of cash for this awesome idea. Or we can work out the details later. Or else, you could have somebody else, like a real writer, write it, and maybe send me a free copy. Or at least pull some strings at the library so I could get up on the waiting list?

If you're not interested in *The Diary of Anne Frankenstein* we could talk about *M__y Dick*. But I need something, please and soon.

I look forward to hearing from you.

Sincerely,

Pete Maynard

Bear Country

MY SON'S FIRST WORD WAS "PANDA;" HIS FIRST SENTENCE: "LOOK AT the bear." "Panda" was recognizable if a little drawn out, the syllables broken in the wrong place. Paaaaa-nduh. "Look at the bear" sounded more like "lookadubba," so it took me a minute to decode, especially because he said it while pointing at an illustration of a stuffed kangaroo.

My first reaction to each was pride. He'd said the word at ten months, the sentence at fifteen, neither with any prompting from either my wife or myself. There had been many other words in the months between, some to be expected — daddy, mommy, yes, no, hurt — others, like hedgehog, helicopter, jaguar, leviathan, a little more of a surprise. But as I closed the book I'd been reading him, the one with the kangaroo, which was actually about various kinds of light — streetlamps, lightning bugs, lightning itself — I realized that my son's vocabulary, though impressive, would not help much with anything he was likely to encounter in everyday life, now or in the future.

As I lowered his warm, sleeping body into the crib, I considered how few of the things we'd been reading about, mostly from books my own father and mother had read to me, I'd ever seen in person. I have never, for example, laid eyes on a giant panda. Having only known them through pictures, I don't have a good idea of a panda's size. Are they larger, on average, than the bigger dogs? Take St. Bernards. You don't see them often, either, and never with small rum barrels hanging from their necks, though children's books depict St. Bernards frequently, and always with the barrel. How many animals in a common alphabetical bestiary had I personally encountered? Camels and elephants and orangutans, yes, but only on trips to the zoo. I doubt I know a single person who has swum with a narwhal or petted a yak. All this is to say nothing of the sentient train engines; the sentient cabooses that use their brakes on steep mountains to save non-sentient engines. I don't even know if trains have cabooses anymore. I doubt that there ever was, but I know that there never will be another train that, smiling, says, "Chugga-chugga-choo-choo."

By the time I climbed into bed beside my already-sleeping wife, I was deep into wondering whether the disconnect between what children's books had led me to expect and what life turned out to be might be at the root of the sense of disappointment that nags at me, as it seems to nag at everyone I come across, whenever I'm not simply crushed under the weight of an overwhelming sadness.

I lay on my back staring up at the ceiling fan and remembered that the fan had been my son's first friend, remembered how he'd giggled and babbled as the fan spun, blowing its cool air down on him during that first hot summer of his life. Except for his milkings, they were the purest, most joyful interactions I had ever witnessed. It gave me an idea for how I would revolutionize children's stories, childhood in general, and, by extension, adult life.

***

At the office this morning I looked around for subjects that could serve as the basis for this new form of children's education. A stapler that does not smile or speak with you, but does, when pressed firmly, make a pleasant clacking sound, ejecting a set of fang-like brackets into a stack of paper unless it's too thick. A computer that does, in a sense, speak to, if not with, you, though it never says anything you want to hear. A supervisor who speaks with you rather too much, who says everything you want to hear, except that the promotion has come through, that the company is aware that it's been working you too hard, that it has finally realized that you are no rock from which to squeeze every last drop of blood. A coworker with whom you have not spoken since the office Christmas party when, having had a few too many per, you exchanged some awkward and even painful gropes, of whom you have lived in fear since that day, though the gropes were mutual, consensual, and she is probably as afraid of you as etc.

As the possibilities for imbuing the quotidien with beauty, for my son, for myself, for all people, slipped away, from me, from us, so did my nagging sense of disappointment, making room for the overwhelming feeling of sadness that bore down on me as insistently as the jaundice light from the overhead fluorescents.

Now that I thought about it, my son's relationship with the fan had not worked out, either. When the weather cooled and we stopped its spinning, he had spent hours, then days, screaming at it, begging it to breathe on him again. Now he never looks at it; he barely ever even looks up.

I placed my forehead on my deskplanner, and tried to weep but could not. I had to stop at the store on the way home.

***

There is no feeling better than the one you get walking through your front door and, stopping in the vestibule, seeing the outline of your toddler son through the frosted glass of the door to the living room and knowing he is there waiting for you. There is nothing more powerful than the moment you inch open that frosted door and, after hanging up your coat and sliding off your shoes, peek through as your boy's eyes brighten with tears of happiness, as his mouth spreads into a goofy, gap-toothed smile and he starts to clap his hands, to applaud, for you, for the very fact that you have arrived home at the same time as you always do. There is no warmer sensation than that of lifting his little body and holding him to your chest when he raises his stubby arms to you, fingers outstretched and wriggling. There is no greater joy than to feel his hot breath on your cheek, his bird-like pulse between his temple and yours.

Or so I used to think.

It is so much more powerful to step through the front door and see him through the frosted glass, standing there, waiting. But instead of cracking the door as soon as you've hung up your coat, to unpack the box from the costume store as carefully and quietly as possible, to slide the costume over your department store suit while your son tries to figure out what's going on on the other side of the glass, to pull the massive, surprisingly realistic grizzly bear's head over your own as your son begins to back away, and, realizing that the paws of your costume will make it impossible to turn the knob, and that to remove your paw, turn the knob, and replace it will ruin the effect, to crash through the frosted glass with a roar you didn't know you were capable of as your son runs screaming through the house, hitting his pale, smooth head with his tiny, impossibly soft fists and running into furniture, fixtures, walls, until he finds his mother's arms, though the screaming does not cease for a long time after.

The boy is finally asleep, the mess is cleaned up, and my wife is still angry. The costume will go back to the shop tomorrow, and the door is going to be expensive to replace. But this is only the beginning. I'm already thinking about an outfit that will involve a shriner's cap, a shiny black wig, some swim goggles, a welder's apron, and a pair of rubber kitchen gloves, probably pink, so that I will not have to shatter glass. Next time, at least.

When I will do it depends on the boy: Does he still believe in Santa Claus? Has he been giggling or groaning in his sleep? When was the last time he waved hello to an inanimate object?

I can't, and don't want to, ensure that he won't know sadness, but he won't know mine. I'll be a goddamned unicorn on the first day of school. At his confirmation, I'll descend from the cathedral's vaulted ceiling, a stigmatic dove crowned with thorns. I'll be a dead girl in a letterman's jacket on prom night. For his wedding reception, I'll buy jarred fetuses on eBay, arrange them semicircle, and, with a series of electrical pulses, make them perform a graceless and complicated dance.

I love my son with such a deep, dark, ghastly love, that when I die, hopefully when he is much older than I am now, for his sake, not mine, I will haunt him like some specimen from the deepest, most gorgeous pit of hell.

One to No One

IT ISN'T ALL CIA WITH THESE CRAZIES. It's not like on *Law and Order* where the schizo thinks he's on the run from some Bernie Madoff proxies who might have connections to an international art theft ring which is clearly just a front for a Sonoran cartel which, combined with several Lichtensteinian banks and the Lubavitchers, forms the shadowy triumvirate that average working stiffs, and even the lower- and middle-levels of the shadow organization itself, merely sense in the back of their heads as the New World Order. As if that explains why he has to rape his grandma or slit open his uncle's belly and make a home in his guts.

Believe me, there are nuts who don't think they're the pillar Atlas is standing on when he shrugs. Some of them are pretty harmless.

Take this hag sitting in the booth across from my table in the Potbelly Sandwich Works at the corner of 12th and Walnut on Saturday, September 25, 2010. Sure, she's grumpy and ugly, but she isn't going to hurt anybody, hasn't yet and never will.

Her thing is that she's a famous crooner. I know this because she mentioned at 12:15 p.m. that she was scheduled to sing at the Borgata Casino on the Boardwalk in Atlantic City tomorrow night, and then she mentioned it again at 1:07. In between she mixed metaphors about how the Industry wants to fuck you in the ass and spit you out and some other things that I missed because she wasn't talking to me and because I got caught up trying to picture someone personifying the Industry fucking her in the ass and spitting her out. The Industry as I imagine it looks something like a late-middle-aged Frankie Avalon, but with an even shinier suit, tanner skin, bigger, whiter teeth.

The guy she's talking to looks nothing like Frankie Avalon. In fact he looks like he crawled out of the same gutter she did and is probably her common-law husband. As far as I can tell, this is the only flaw in her whole delusion, because she's incorporated the other possible pitfalls seamlessly into the delusion itself.

Her look, for example. She looks like a fucking bag lady on the government dole. Big sweatpants, ratty T-shirt, and a wig that couldn't pass for real hair with Ray Charles at twenty yards, dead or alive. Real stars usually opt for a ballcap and glasses instead of a mop, but I have seen them in wigs, and otherwise that's exactly the way they dress when they want you to notice them. It's their way of saying, "Look, I'm regular people, like you. I'm just so used to wearing star clothes I can't quite get it right."

See, star clothes, real star clothes, are too much for the human brain to process. They require the mediation of cameras to be seen. Think about it — Lady Gaga is walking by you pretty much every single day in a dress made of kitten meat and depleted uranium, but you'll never catch it with your naked eye. You don't even notice you were standing right behind her up on Front and Girard on

May 17, 2010 or whatever, until you see the picture in the glossy pages of *Us Magazine* a month or so later.

She was just outside the McDonald's, wearing some kind of rubber S and M harness with a rotting banana where the black leather dildo should be, and if you squint you can see it's you looking normal in jeans, a sweater, and tennis shoes caught in the act of turning back around when you were already on your way out because you realized that, yes, that was Zooey Deschanel in plaid pajama bottoms, plastic thong flipflops, and a ketchup-stained wifebeater sans bra posing for snapshots with patrons in front of the soda fountain.

In other words, Zooey Deschanel: fame whore; Lady Gaga: avoiding attention at all costs, even of her dignity.

It was the same with Madonna in the eighties. The nineteen eighties. Because now that she's in her own eighties she needs attention, which is why she walks around looking like she could be a close friend of this lady here in the Potbelly, who, okay, maybe there are a couple cases where she takes the look too far. There's the no teeth thing. I'm not saying all stars have all their teeth, but I am saying you don't see them around the way without their falsies in. On the other hand, no teeth seems like it might be good for blowjobs, and if the sex tapes have taught us anything it's that celebrities love blowjobs and are excellent at them.

I get caught up staring at the quivering hole in her face until she mentions the big Borgata show again and I have to snap out of it and listen for if there are any more details.

The concert at the Borgata is the second potential flaw in her delusion. Not the concert itself, but how close she's scheduled it. Tomorrow. It's a risk, like when Prince predicted 1999 was going to be this big party and then everyone was just home alone watching the Marx Brothers marathon on new year's rockin' eve, or all those preachers who had to change the date of the millennium when Jesus didn't come back in the year 2000.

What most people would do is be like Orson Welles and make the prediction for a long time after you're dead, so that when 1984 rolls around and not only is everything not a post-apocalyptic communist piece of shit, it's actually better than it's ever been, all of it, and a movie star is president, no one bothers to blame you or at least you don't hear it because your ears have rotted along with the rest of you.

The other thing you could do is get it right, like the Mayans with 2012, but this lady is no Mayan, and she will never be playing the Borgata, and here's the thing: this is not the first time, or I should say the first four times since she just mentioned it again, that I've heard her say she was playing the Borgata tomorrow.

The first time was when I first got to town back in 2007. I don't remember the exact date and time because I wasn't really paying attention, but it was probably late July, early evening, a weekday, and it was definitely in the Burger King at 8th and Chestnut which I remember because that particular restaurant is located between a subway stop and a hospital, which makes it basically a magnet for sickness and crazy, so when she stood up and announced to the whole restaurant that she was playing the Borgata tomorrow, I barely even noticed.

Then came Saturday, January 5, 2008, at the Starbucks on 15th between Spruce and Locust. 3:04 p.m. She was with this skinny black man who was not trying to hide the fact that he kept reaching into his busted backpack to pull out a bottle of Vladimir that he was dumping into his tall paper cup of breakfast blend. I don't need to tell you it was not Sammy Davis, Jr. Sammy Davis, Jr. was dead by then. This guy only smelled dead.

The hag was going on and on about the price of fame, how, and this is verbatim, I wrote it down, "the hoi polloi won't leave you alone long enough to take a shit, but the bastards that run the studios, they act like they never knew you once they get what they want, if you know what I mean."

The black guy didn't seem to know what she meant. He was the hoi polloi.

She pointed toward her caved-in mouth as she sputtered the syllables. "Their nice little wives don't give blowjobs."

Suddenly her mouth sagged even more and so did the rest of her face. It was like she'd just realized that she'd been whoring herself for fame all these years. Or else she realized she hadn't. It was a little hard to tell, even for me.

"There's got to be a bright side," said the hoi polloi.

He pushed his drink toward her. She brightened up. At first it looked like she'd brightened up about the drink, but she didn't take a sip, not then, not the whole time I was there. Maybe it was the fact he'd offered. Then again, maybe it was the thought of the show at the Borgata, because she said: "There's the show at the Borgata."

The hoi polloi nodded, pulled the drink back toward himself, took a sip.

"The Borgata," he said.

"The lights," she said, "the music, the applause," she said. "It makes it all worthwhile."

"Tomorrow," said the hoi polloi.

"Tomorrow," she said.

Of course I knew there was no show at the Borgata tomorrow. Rather, there was a show scheduled at the Borgata, and all I had to do was go out to the corner and grab a copy of the *City Paper* to prove to myself and her if I felt like it that it was not her playing a show that night but James Taylor or the New Kids on the Block or Kid Rock. (I did check later. It was Jim Gaffigan, who does not even sing.) What I wanted to know was how she would deal with that. What would happen if she went all the way to the Borgata only to find that not only did she not have a show, but that they wouldn't even let her smelly ass through the front door?

But no. But no, of course not. She wasn't going to Atlantic City, and I didn't have to go there to know that. All I had to do was make the rounds of the Center City fast food franchises. I started around 5:00 p.m. at the McDonald's in Rittenhouse, then worked my way through the foodcourt at Liberty Place, Dunkin' Donuts on Chestnut between 15th and 16th, then the Wendy's at the corner. I decided to skip over the other Dunkin' Donuts because none of the ones in the neighborhood have seating areas, and also the Bellevue, because it's too high class, and checked in at the Wendy's at 12th and Chestnut where I did not find her but did have dinner around 6:15. Five-piece nugget, dollar fries, and Coke. From there I worked my way north to the McDonald's at 10th and Market and then to the food court at the Gallery Mall where I finally found her in front of the Chick-fil-a which was closed, it being a Sunday.

There she was with her wig, without teeth, with a cup of Burger King coffee on the table before her and another man across. The guy's clothes looked worn but clean enough, his hair shiny with grease but close-cut. He had a faded, prison-style tattoo on his forehead that said "Maid in America," which I think is a typo.

I got my own cup of coffee and took a seat at the table next to them. I couldn't make out a word they were saying. The guy was a mumbler and the hag was toothless and the food court was loud and echoey.

I tried to remind myself that the point was she didn't have a show that night at the Borgata and I had proven the point to myself, but I didn't feel like I had accomplished anything except to waste three hours and five dollars of my life because deep down I'd known damn well that she didn't have a show at the Borgata, and what I wanted to know was how she'd rationalize saying she did.

I sat there staring at my coffee trying to tune into the frequency she and the American-maid man were speaking on, but I only caught a couple of words. "Heartless bastards," I think. Maybe "grammy." Without context I couldn't guess whether she was talking about the National Academy of Recording Arts and Sciences or her mother's mother.

Finally I took my tepid coffee, downed it in one thick, clammy sip, slammed the paper cup down, and stood up facing her table. She and her friend went on talking as though I wasn't there, and I couldn't hear them any better standing over them.

"Excuse me," I said, trying to hide my frustration, to sound both polite and confident at the same time.

Maid in America turned toward me first, as though I'd been trying to get his attention when really I couldn't have cared less about him. People are like that. Everyone thinks everyone else revolves around them. Everyone's a star.

"What?" he said.

He didn't lunge, but I could sense the potential energy behind his tattoo, between his shoulders.

"I have a question for your — "

I was trying to think of the right word when the old hag said, "yes," dismissively, almost aristocratic. It was such an impressive imitation of a star, especially directed at someone, me, who had found her out, who had the power to expose her, although she couldn't know it yet, that it took me a second to pull myself together.

"Excuse me," I said again.

"Yes," she said again.

"Do you have a show at the Borgata tonight?" I said.

She said: "tomorrow," without missing a beat, as though this happened all the time.

As I walked away I couldn't help but marvel at the simple brilliance of it. The show was not that night but tomorrow, not Monday, January 7, 2008, but tomorrow. Always tomorrow and never today. That way, even if someone asked her the date of her next show at the Borgata, she could answer tomorrow. Of course, someone, me, for example, could have asked her: "Are you playing the Borgata tomorrow, as in January 7?" but that would sound unnatural, and she would recognize it for a trap and probably just answer "tomorrow."

I felt like I'd been outwitted, then and for a long time after, and I did not see her again until today. It was almost as if she'd been avoiding me. But seeing her here in the Potbelly I realize that she hasn't been thinking about me at all, that she *still* isn't thinking about me at all.

Frankly, I am not okay with that. It's not exactly a flaw in her delusion, but it shows a lack of grace, which, as everyone knows, is one of the star qualities. You're allowed, even expected, to treat your public with a certain disdain, the disdain befitting your station, but public is the operative word here. The public, as in the hoi polloi, as in, not the people who have you all figured out, even if said people admire the facade you've built. And I do admire the facade, but now I've found a structural flaw, and it's these guys she spends her time with. It's these fucking guys. It's this guy sitting across from her.

He's wearing a cheap wig, too, but his is short and blond, and I bet he'd call it a toupee if you could get him to acknowledge it. I bet he woke up in her bed this morning after a night of gummy blowjobs and ass fucking and outspitting and she was already finishing up her toilette. I bet she walked in from the bathroom, or more likely turned around from the kitchenette sink of her Section 8 efficiency, to find him stirring beneath the sheets, and asked him: "Where shall we go today? McDonald's? Taco Bell? The Potbelly?" and he smiled contentedly and said: "The Borgata, maybe?" and she told him: "The Borgata's tomorrow, silly!" so he settled for Potbelly, jumping out of bed already full dressed in those nasty pleated khakis, the mangy summer sweater crumpled over his torso, even the duct-taped New Balances on his feet, saying "Just let me get my toupee on" as he lifts it off of the avocado-shaped bedpost and adjusts it over his wispy head.

That's him. That's her Frankie Avalon. For Christ's sake his shirttail is sticking out of his fly, and what I want to know is how does she get around it? I can see her looking in the mirror and still managing to convince herself that she's a star, never going to the Borgata but never doubting that the show must and will go on, even being ignored if not treated like some stinking waste of life by every single person she passes on the street and telling herself that the disguise is working. But how does she sit across from that pathetic skeleton draped in moldy clothes and not want to find a set of false teeth if only so that she can try to gnaw open the veins in her wrist and finally put an end to the whole fucking farce? How can she gum his nubby dick, lie beneath him as he pumps it in and out, and caress his skin, which is like cheese under Reynold's wrap? How can she sit across from that nobody and still believe she's anybody?

And who does she think she is, anyway?

Something I haven't considered before. For instance, does she just use her real name? Like if her name is Sally Simpson, a name that would be hard and gross to pronounce with no teeth, does she operate as though Sally Simpson is a star, never questioning why Sally Simpson's name never appears, not just on the marquee of the Borgata, which she's probably never seen, but in the tabloids, on the TV, on *Wikipedia*, though I bet she's never even heard of it? Or has she appropriated another star's identity, an actual star— Liza Minelli, Liz Taylor, Loni Anderson?

My money's on Shirley Temple. She's got grown-up, used-up nymphet written all over every inch of what sagging skin I can see. I wish I could examine the rest of her to make sure. But that won't do, not in the middle of the Potbelly Sandwich Works on 12th and Walnut.

But there is something I can do even now. I'm not one of these guys she rolls around with who doesn't question tomorrow. I can take this copy of the *City Paper* I've been sitting here pretending to read for the past three hours, open to a page of advertisements featuring the major events at the Borgata for the next several weeks. I can stand up and walk over to her table. I can slam that paper down in front of her and demand something, an explanation, her attention, her autograph.

Yes, an autograph. That's what I'll do.

"Excuse me, " I say, "I'm practically your biggest fan and I'm just shocked to find you here at this Potbelly restaurant, at any Potbelly at all, even in this sorry excuse for a city, and though, at the moment, I don't have any of the many glossy headshots spanning your entire career that I usually carry close to my heart everywhere I go, I know that you often grace the stage of the Borgata, and so I found this advertisement for the Borgata here in the *City Paper*, and I wondered if you'd sign it for me."

She looks at me kind of stunned, but then her face collapses into something like a smile and says "Of course," she says, "anything for a fan."

She starts digging around in her bag, for a pen I think. Not very star-like, not carrying around a pen, a writing implement of some sort, preferably a Sharpie so the signature doesn't smudge on shiny paper. I reach into my pocket and pull one out, always ready, and hand it to her.

"Thank you," she says. "To whom should I make it out?"

I don't miss a beat. I tell her: "The Ultimate Warrior."

"A beautiful name," she says, "exotic," and she writes it down, slowly, dutifully, in her third-grader's script, covering the better part of the page and bleeding through and tearing the cheap newsprint in some places.

When she finally hands it back she's got a tear in her eye and I say "thank you" and she says "thank you," choking up a little like maybe this is something she doesn't do every day, like maybe I've made her week if not her life. I read it in front of her. Not out loud, but I stand there and decipher her scrawl in silence:

"Dearest The Ultimate Warrior," it says. "There's always a bright side."

But there isn't a bright side, because the signature below it is an illegible tangle of loops and slashes that couldn't possibly add up to a name, famous or otherwise, and anyway, she's definitely a nutcase and a fraud, no real star, because I can see it on her face — she doesn't recognize me, my face, my facepaint, my tassels, my name, and everybody knows it takes one to know one.

The Myth of the Myth of Sisyphus

FRAG AND WATT WILL NEVER GIVE UP ON THE GHOST ENGINE, BUT they haven't thought of it in several hours or worked on it in as many days. Frag has ceded Watt the wrench, has come to see it as writing tool rather than weapon, because, of late, Watt has taken to drawing lines in the sand, lines shaped like letters, letters that would add up to words if only a bird's eye view were possible, if only a plane or a chopper or a goddamned god would fly over wherever this is. Frag in turn has claimed the rag. He is done wasting time with words; he's dedicated himself to physical fitness, to keeping his body lean and hard. In this heat, the rag makes a fine chamois towel.

There they are—scribbling, squatting, thrusting—when the engine sputters to something like life. It begins with a series of slow, dry spurts, and builds soon enough to a dull, concussive chug, the kind you'd associate with an operational engine. Now its chrome pipe pumps a thick steam toward the heavens, alternate green and pink pastels, puff-by-puff.

Frag is first to notice. The work of the body is exhausting, requires frequent rest. Pausing to wipe the sweat from his brow, he chances a glance at the sky, then follows the colorful smoke to its source: the Ghost Engine.

"Watt," he says.

"What?" says Watt, bent over his composition.

Frag says: "Look."

Watt looks at Frag. Frag is looking up. Watt looks where Frag is looking, finally sees the beautiful pink and green cloud forming in the bright blue sky. He gets to his feet, hesitant, hopeful and yet suspicious. He still has the presence of mind to shove the wrench by its handle between the waistband of his pants and the skin of his back, snug, before the smoke cools, condenses, begins to sprinkle both the men and their surroundings with a gorgeous, glistening mist.

Have you ever twisted and turned a thirty-four foot travel trailer up the Pacific Coast Highway while early Enya warbles from the cassette deck of your conversion van?

Have you emerged from a passenger train into the hold of a freight ship and climbed to the top deck to leap and spin above the North Sea beneath midnight stars?

How many times has your spouse paused from work to stand on hands against the wall reciting explicit rap lyrics, and was the sex that night top-ten?

If you have never experienced any of these particular phenomena but are starting to get an idea of what the narrative is gesturing toward, which is moments of unexpected ecstasy, sudden fleeting bliss, and you have had such a happy accident of your own, take a moment to remember.

Relive it.

Good.

Now imagine the feel of machine drizzle on your bare skin

after so much failure, and understand why Watt and Frag dance.

Now picture their world this afternoon beneath its sheen of green and pink as the Ghost Engine's exhaust blocks the sun.

Now imagine, understand, and picture how it will go when the motor chokes and dies with as little warning as it started.

Frag and Watt stand motionless in a tight hug as the last of the machine drool smears the flesh of their torsos. The cloud is gone already, the sun bright again, and baking. Watt feels sweat replacing mist, attempts to disengage, but Frag holds him firm. It isn't fellow feeling. Frag's fingers tickle toward Watt's waistband, the wrench. Watt twists his hips, gets the wrench out of range. Frag tries to follow, first with his fingers, and when that fails, his arms, his shoulders. Eventually he tries to lock Watt's legs with his own. They struggle in circles, silent but for grunts of exertion, both knowing the stakes, neither acknowledging them with anything but his body.

Finally Frag lunges, grabs the grip, shoves Watt with his other arm, and the wrench comes free.

Watt anticipates a drubbing. He squats, covers his arms with his head, cowers. It is full minutes before he decides that the blows aren't coming, or not now. He peaks between spread fingers, finds Frag busy at the Ghost Engine, frantically tightening bolts and buffing the body. The sun has evaporated all evidence of the Ghost Engine's recent functioning; the landscape is back to its customary drab.

Watt creeps toward Frag, catches snatches of syllables between Frag's frantic panting. "Please … (huff) … God … (huff) … Funk," Frag seems to say.

Funk? Watt thinks. That can't be right. Frag needs a reset. Watt presses the button, that concave at the base of the skull. He lands an elbow just above the neck, good and fast, so Frag won't know what's happened.

When Frag comes to, Watt is seated beside him, hunched and rubbing the back of his neck to give the impression that they've both been hammered by the same invisible arm, that Frag just happened to get the worst of it.

"You, too, huh?" says Frag.

Watt grimaces. The grimace isn't a lie, exactly, but it succeeds in misleading. He feels bad for his friend. It was he who made his friend feel bad, of course, but only because it had to happen. The wrench is back where it belongs, between Watt's waist and waistband, spanner covered by a T-shirt but protuberant like a tail.

"There is no God," he says, "nor any funk."

"What's funk got to do with it?" says Frag.

"Nothing, is what I'm saying," Watt says. "One must imagine Sisyphus happy, after all."

"Must one?" says Frag.

Watt has never heard his friend Frag sound so incurious, so unbelligerent. It's a chance, he thinks, to win the day.

"He *is* condemned by the gods to roll that rock to the top of a mountain, only to have it roll back down each time. If the goal is to plant the rock at the top —"

"Why should that be the goal?" says Frag.

"What," says Watt, "the middle?"

"Maybe the goal is to be pushing a rock," Frag says. "Couldn't he take a toddler's delight in watching it roll back down?"

"Sisyphus," says Watt, "is not a toddler, and even if he could access the toddler's mindset, he does not have the toddler's freedom to walk away. He would certainly despair each time he started again from the bottom, unless he were, as we are imagining him, happy."

"Speak for yourself," says Frag.

There's no question now: Frag is frustrated, maybe to the point of resignation. Watt feels large, full only of himself.

"In speaking for myself, I speak for us all."

"Then speak for us all about the size of the hill," says Frag. "It's a large one?"

"A very large hill," says Watt. "A very heavy boulder."

"Remember TeBordo's novel?" Frag says. "The one where the boy receives email from his mother's account after her death? Free movie tickets, uncollected lottery winnings, mortgage upgrades and the like. Must we imagine TeBordo's mother happy as she presses send on an offer of erectile enhancement pills from beyond the grave?"

Something is off here; Watt had Frag up that hill with the boulder, and now Frag is being an ass.

"You're being an ass," he says.

"It really happened, you know," says Frag. "The emails. She managed to send a postcard, too, but TeBordo left it out. Worried it would muddy the narrative waters."

Watt looks at Frag; Frag isn't looking Watt's way. Watt grabs the wrench, lets it rest between his thighs with a loose hand on the handle.

"Camus concerns himself with Sisyphus in *The Myth of Sisyphus*," he says.

It sounds like whining, even to him.

"And now you're concerning yourself with Camus concerning himself with Sisyphus," Frag says.

"Only as a way of concerning myself with Camus's fundamental question," says Watt.

"Which is?" says Frag.

"Whether or not to go on living," Watt says. "Camus begins his essay by saying that, and I quote, there is only one really serious philosophical question, and that is suicide, end-quote."

"And you've concluded that if you can imagine Sisyphus happy you can go on pushing your own rock," says Frag.

"I don't flatter myself quite so tragic as Sisyphus," Watt says.

"The Sisyphus to be found in Book XI of the *Odyssey*?" says Frag.

"The only Sisyphus I recognize," Watt says.

"And the others Odysseus meets in Book XI," says Frag, "Must one imagine *them* happy, too?"

Watt is drawing lines again. He doesn't know when it started, didn't make the choice, but the handle is dragging back and forth like a sand-slowed pendulum.

"Maybe they're *all* happy," he says.

"If they are, they have an odd way of expressing it," says Frag. "They don't have bodies. No hugs, even from dear mom. They have to drink from the arteries of oxen just to be heard. Everyone Odysseus speaks with asks him why he's come to the gloomy dark of this joyless place, and then they exchange words of sadness while grieving and shedding tears. Until Achilles shows up and laps the black blood."

"He's unhappy, too," says Watt.

"Emphatically unhappy," says Frag. "When Odysseus tells him to look on the bright side of Hades, Achilles says, and now I myself will quote, Don't try to reconcile me to my dying. I'd rather serve as another man's laborer, as a poor peasant without land, and be alive on Earth, than be lord of all the lifeless dead, end quote. Meanwhile, Sisyphus is silent."

"So we must imagine Sisyphus *un*happy," says Watt.

"The Greeks could not have imagined him otherwise," says Frag, "but if you wish to live in bad faith, I'm not going to insist. There is only one must when it comes to imagining Sisyphus."

"How must I imagine Sisyphus?" says Watt.

"You must imagine Sisyphus dead," Frag says. "As dead as I'll make you if you ever so much as think about hitting my reset button again."

They aren't just lines. Watt has been writing, and because he's been writing between his feet, which are planted firmly in the sand, he alone has a bird's-eye view of the message: Please. God. Funk.

"Then who will save us?" he says.

Frag is first to laugh. Watt laughs, too, but he doesn't laugh last, because Frag is still at it when his towel-wrapped fist lands hard on Watt's head.

The American Family Robinson

THAT SUMMER THE FORESTS SURROUNDING OUR TOWN WERE LEVELED by fires, and the air was so saturated with smoke and ash that your face got streaked with soot the moment you stepped outside. The soot smudged with sweat in the heat, even if you were only walking to the mailbox and back, and your mouth was full with a taste like muddy toast whether you left the house or not, no matter how many times you brushed your teeth and tongue.

Most of the neighbors went to stay with relatives in other towns and states; others checked into hotels and campgrounds far from the fires, but Mom and Dad refused to leave, because, they said, we had nowhere else to go.

Really, though, they seemed to be enjoying themselves. Dad took up painting, muraled the walls of our finished basement with a tropical scene that betrayed a lack of training and the fact that he'd never been to the tropics. Beneath a dense canopy of palms and what looked like the birches burning just beyond our neighborhood, a monkey clutching a mango rode a crocodile bareback, while a vulture lunged from a thick branch, its beak eager for the rattlesnake slithering up the trunk.

Mom dragged the dog's house from the backyard into ours,

hung drywall inside of it to divide the space into a living room, a bedroom, a bath, furnished it with pieces from an old dollhouse I'd abandoned to my sister who'd abandoned it to a closet. When she was finished, the thing was wildly out of scale and not even the smallest dog would have fit inside, but it didn't matter, because our dog, which had not been small at all, had died three summers earlier.

My sister and I enjoyed ourselves less. I would have imagined I'd be the one to take it harder. I was fifteen, had friends, a boyfriend. They'd all left, and I couldn't help imagining them recreating my social life without me in a setting not unlike the one Dad's mural depicted. My sister, on the other hand, was a homebody, her gangliness somehow ganglier than that of the average twelve-year-old. Her plans for the summer, if you could call them plans, consisted of reading several books a day, letting those teen romances about tragic first love, suicide, and hitchhiking prom queen ghosts, stand in for a life she was not yet ready, might never be ready to live.

I didn't understand why she couldn't just keep her plans under the circumstances, couldn't understand how the smell of the smoke changed her situation at all, but she seemed to grow skinnier, paler, more awkward each day. When the power finally went out and we realized the phone lines were down, she fainted like the heroine of an eighteenth-century novel.

By the time we got her revived and lying on the couch with her feet up, my father seemed even happier than before.

"We can pretend like we're completely cut off from the outside world," he said, "pioneer settlers on an undiscovered continent."

"Atlantis," said my mother.

"The American Family Robinson," said my father. He told my

sister: "You could be the one to tell our story."

Nothing he might have said could have made me feel worse. Before the power had gone out, I'd felt like we were on another planet, but even interplanetary explorers needed electricity, air conditioning. We couldn't open the windows because of the smoke, and the air inside the house was already hot and thick and stifling. It seemed to make my sister feel better. Once she was strong enough to get up from the couch, she went to her room and rearranged her desk, lined up paper, pencils, erasers, prepared to tell the story of the American Family Robinson.

Later that night, I stood on the back deck and watched my parents swim naked in the pool by the light of the not-too-distant fires. Animals scurried from wood to wood across the lawn. Flames flickered between patches and masses of smoke. It looked like someone had uprooted the Garden of Eden and grafted it onto hell. My mother broke the surface of the water, arching her back, and tossing her head. A shower of sprinkles flew from her long, dark hair like sparks. My father swam over to embrace her, and I couldn't take it any longer. I had never seen them so happy.

In her room, my sister sat facing the window, hunched over her desk, scribbling our story, or her version of it, I assumed, by candlelight. I stood in her doorway and tried to clear my throat to get her attention, but my throat was dry from the smoke and I ended up hacking until my eyes watered and my stomach muscles ached. When I looked up I saw that she'd turned to face me.

"Are you okay?" she said.

"I'm okay," I said.

I was as okay as I could be under the circumstances. But she seemed to be doing better than okay, better than I'd seen her in a long time, before the fires, even. There was some color in her face, and she'd already started to fill out a little.

"Okay," she said.

She turned around, lifted a sheet of paper covered in her bubbly girl handwriting, and held the edge to the candle's flame. Once the paper caught, she dropped it into the metal wastebasket beside her desk where it joined others like it to judge by the smoke and ashes that floated above the rim. She took a pencil from a jar and held it over a clean sheet.

I stepped into her room as she began to write again. I was curious what she was up to, and maybe jealous that she'd found a way to fill her time.

"I've been thinking," I said.

"Yeah," she said, pencil scratching slowly.

"The world's ending," I said, "and Mom and Dad have lost it."

I watched the back of her head bob, nodding or just bouncing to the rhythm of her writing. I took a couple of steps toward her.

"If we make it through this it'll be up to us to start over," I said.

She stopped writing and turned around, but didn't say anything. I took two more steps her way. I was close enough to reach out and put my fingertips on her shoulder, but I didn't.

"We'll have to repopulate the world," I said. "I'm older," I said, "so I'll be the husband."

As I said it, I watched her expression go from one of mild annoyance, like her silly sister was distracting her from her life's work, to the kind of frightened anxiety I remembered seeing on her face when she was a toddler and realized she'd done something very wrong. She knew she'd done something wrong.

The pencil fell from her hand and hit the carpet with a small, sharp pop. I bent down to get it for her, but by the time I got back up she was standing, and then she was running past me. I heard her feet on the stairs and the front door slamming.

I stood there a minute looking at the pencil, and then I staggered to the window and watched her running, from what and toward what I didn't know; the only thing for her to get away from was our house, us, me, and wherever you ran that summer you were running toward the flames.

I started to look down at the paper on her desk. I wanted to know what she'd written, but for some reason I grabbed the sheet without looking, held it to the candle, and dropped it into the basket.

We never found her, and for a long time we assumed she'd been lost in the fire that somehow spared our neighborhood. Eventually we accepted this, and things went back to something like a routine, if not normal. But then, years later, after I'd moved across the country and started my life anew, I received a postcard from somewhere in Oklahoma. It was written in a simple script I didn't recognize, and there was no signature. It said: "I am no one's wife."

Even after all those years of forgetting I knew right away who'd sent it, as I later knew who sent the ones that came from New York, Tunisia, Algiers, and Tibet.

I am no one's wife.

I am no one's wife.

I am no one's wife.

I am no one's wife.

My only question was whether she was answering my final suggestion, or repeating what she'd written on that last piece of paper. Why she would have been writing that on that smoky summer evening, I can't guess, but I can't guess why she would have run, either. She had to have known I was joking, that no two girls could repopulate the world.

Now that I'm older and have a family of my own, a husband and two daughters, and a house with a yard and a pool, I often sit by the window on a hot summer night and imagine fire surrounding our neighborhood. But instead of inviting my husband out for a swim or checking in on the girls as they sleep, I picture myself walking down the stairs and out the front door. I see myself following the crackle and hiss into the forest until I find my sister towering above it all, clothed in a blaze, and she reaches down to lift the ring of fire from around my little world and slips it onto my tiny finger, igniting my gown in flames.

9/12 in Parts Unknown

HE'D SEEN THE TOWERS FALL BEFORE, SOMETIMES IN PERSON, sometimes on screen, other times in dreams. The big, buzz-cut peckerwood in prison guard's garb taking a dropkick to the chest and crashing flat to the mat; the fat white mongoloid in a muu-muu meant to signify an African heritage that his pigment gave the lie to—flying clothesline to the throat, back against ropes that couldn't support his bulk, the headfirst tumble to the concrete beyond the ring.

But these towers were different. Steel and glass. And then steel and glass and fuel and fire, and tiny bodies trickling few and slow like the last drops from a dead spigot.

Along with every other red-blooded American from Wall Street to Main Street to Parts Unknown, the Ultimate Warrior mourned on September 11, 2001. He trembled; he raged; he wept until his facepaint was hussy-smudged and his breath came in halting hiccups. Finally he fell into a deep, dreamless sleep. He woke with the sun the next morning, feeling refreshed.

Dawn Wednesday, he showered and applied fresh paint and tassels, then went out into the forest beyond his backyard, to commune with nature and to meditate on his options.

The forest beyond his backyard was more of a wood, and only a few acres of it were his to roam, the neighbors on all sides being as protective of their land as the Warrior was of his, so he circled the perimeter as though hemmed in by an imaginary wall, and tried to notice different things each time he passed the same spot—a bird now, the tree branch it perched upon the next, maybe later the tree as a whole — by way of making his domain seem more vast, if only to himself, and as a spur to contemplation.

Three paths presented themselves to him. Not geographically. Geographically, there was only the one. So strategically: he could go on as though nothing had happened, he could prepare to defend his own small plot of the nation, or he could take justice into his own hands and avenge his country against whoever was responsible.

He didn't know yet who was responsible, but he had his suspicions just like everyone else.

Going on as though nothing had happened would have been tantamount to burying his head in the sand. Cowardly. No one had ever accused him of being a coward. Path one—out of the question. Not worth a second thought.

The second path was reasonable, but there was the issue of perception. Preparing to defend your property can look a lot like going on as though nothing has happened, especially if you're already, essentially, prepared. He was prepared. He was always prepared. And so, for example, setting up a razorwire fence or impaling the first intruder on a stake as a warning to any others who might come along would have been so much swinging dick with arms like the Warrior's. Worse, it was reasonable. Reasonable wasn't in his nature.

Unfortunately, the last path, going Rambo on the terrorists or Arabs or whatever, wasn't as easy as it would once have been. He assumed there were still a few little warriors whose first thought on seeing that first plane fly into that first tower, or at least the second—tower and plane, not thought—was *how long will it be before the Ultimate Warrior brings his intense brand of punishment to the perpetrators?* In truth, the Warrior was surprised that none of them had shown up on his webforum to ask exactly that the day before. But he wasn't so delusional as to believe the numbers were anything like they would have been back in the good old days.

Why couldn't they, whoever *they* were, have flown a plane into a skyscraper on September 11, 1989, or any day between, say 1988 and 1992. Had they been scared? Of him? No, he knew it wasn't that. But still. As fun as it would have been to go bash some toweled heads, he had kids now and he didn't know how to go about getting the necessary security clearances and he didn't speak a word of Arabic. It had to be Arabic. Who else, Russians?

He'd taken care of some Russians in his prime.

Of course, there was one other path. But no, it wasn't really a path. He couldn't claim responsibility. Not that he didn't have it in him—the ability, the strength—to claim responsibility. He didn't have the desire. It was wrong. The act itself and the taking of responsibility for it when he'd had nothing to do with it.

No matter how much attention it would draw.

He was about to go back inside and check the webforum one more time before the twins got up and he and his wife had to get them off to school, but then he had a better idea: he was out in nature.

He was communing with nature. He could ask nature what to do. She would know.

He stopped beneath the tree he'd passed three times already, the one with the bird in it. But this time he didn't look at the bird or the branch or the tree. This time he stared directly up at the clear blue sky and he spread out his arms, letting his still-formidable biceps flex and twitch a little even though there was no one there but nature to see it, nature and the bird, and he let his mouth fall open and he breathed in the crisp morning air letting it fill his lungs, and then he roared as loud as he could, like in the old days, but more coherent, more focused.

He roared: "What would you have me do?"

The bird cawed or croaked or something. "Mother!" it seemed to say.

He wasn't sure at first, but he thought the feeling flowing through him as he stood on the back patio and reached for the sliding glass door might be peace. A warrior in his prime doesn't know much peace, but he was no longer in his prime, hadn't been for a long time.

He'd been trying to learn peace for years, by communing with nature, with little success. Strange, then, that he should feel it on the morning after such an unpeaceful event. But yes, it was peace. He knew it as the door swished on its track. The sound it made. That soothing sound. September 12 was a new beginning. What those savages had done was despicable, unforgivable, but something good would come from it. You have to tear down the old to build up the new. Nature makes everything new. Nature brings peace.

He was at peace as he stepped onto the soft, thick-pile carpet of his living room and let it tickle his feet, peace as he closed the door behind him and heard again that sublime sound.

He stood just inside a while, his back to the yard, without even a quick glance over his shoulder to be sure that no one had followed him from the forest, that no one was even now crossing his back lawn, intent on shattering his hard-won peace.

Of course, he knew that no one was following him. He had the instincts of a hunter. But the peace was so deep, so, for lack of a better word, *peaceful*, that even having to gut an intruder with his bare paws wouldn't have broken it.

"This peace," he said to the empty living room, "what could break it?"

Not a trespassing assassin.

Not a whole host of the heathen hordes rising up from the east intent on destroying our way of life.

Not a battalion of aliens storming his property on brontosaurs they'd reanimated with the juice that ran their fucking spaceships.

Not even an argument between the girls, his wife shrieking about how they had to get ready for school.

He listened. The twins weren't fighting. No one else in the house was awake. He could tell. It was still early. He could tell that, too. Didn't even have to look at the clock.

He stepped onto the cold linoleum of the kitchen floor, and that was peaceful, too, in its way. And cooking brought peace. He would fix his brood a warrior's breakfast, a feast of scrambled egg whites and hearty, multi-grain toast.

He heard the first stirrings upstairs as he separated the last of the ooze from its yolk and shell and tossed the three empty cartons into the trash. He realized he'd better make coffee. His wife didn't partake, but the girls could get violent if they didn't have at least a couple of mugs each before homeroom.

As he reached for the carafe, he happened to look down at the counter and noticed the answering machine. He still used an answering machine in 2001. He was a believer in the old ways. The tiny red light was blinking on and off, on and off.

Someone had left a message while he'd been out communing with nature. Even in the midst of his mourning the day and night before, even in all of that fear and trembling, he'd kept a close eye on the machine, his ear out for the ring of the phone, just as he'd frequently checked the webforum—in case anyone should try to contact him, anyone wondering what to do, anyone who needed help or advice at a time like this. And all day not a single call, not a single message, not a single post on the boards and only a handful of page views, which might, those last, have come from his frequent checking-in. It was almost as if there was no one out there at all.

He started to feel some of that peace, some of that resolve slipping away.

Why now? A day late and barely after dawn, when the phone's ring could wake his family, get the girls going, the wife hollering.

The peace was gone now, rotting in the trash with three dozen egg shells and their yolks. Now it was a matter of holding back the anger. He clenched his fists and breathed deep—an adenoidal snarl — and began counting in his most seething voice.

One.

Two.

Three.

At eight his wife snuck up behind him, caught him by surprise. "What's got you worked up?" she said.

"Nine," he snarled. "Ten" was barely a whisper, the end of an exhalation, a symbolic release. The anger was still there, but he wouldn't show it, not to his wife. His beautiful wife. He wanted to throw her to the floor and shove his head between her legs until she screamed his trademarked name.

He turned to kiss her good morning. Her face was puffy with sleep and her hair a scraggly mess, but she was still gorgeous. He kissed her swollen cheek at the place where the paint gave way to unadorned flesh. She smiled and reached for the carafe still clenched tight in his right hand. He had trouble letting go, not because he didn't want to—she made coffee as well as he did—but because his hand was almost paralyzed around the plastic handle. He opened it slowly and his knuckles ached.

"You trying to make coffee or strangle the pot?" she said, grinning.

He looked down at his palm, ridged deep with the handle's imprint, then tried to hide it behind his back.

"I'll finish the eggs," he said.

Finish, he'd said. But he hadn't started them yet. They were just a mass of quivering, translucent goo in a stainless steel bowl.

"Good," she said, "the girls'll be down soon."

The girls weren't bad at breakfast. Very little breakage. A little more hairpulling. He hadn't paid much attention, let his wife take care of it, which was unfair, he knew. Some of the pulled hair was hers.

He'd been distracted. He'd realized, as he shoveled mounds of now solid but unseasoned egg whites onto his daughter's plates, that whoever had left that message might not have meant any offense by calling so early, might not have been calling early wherever he or she was from. There were little warriors in other lands, lands where the sun was bright when Parts Unknown was dark, little warriors who needed his guidance at a time like this, a time that transcended time zones.

And what about New York? *The City*, he called it. *Gotham. The twenty-first century Babylon*. There were warriors there still, he knew; he was sure; he could tell by the IP addresses. What there was not was phone service, at least in some parts of the island, from some service providers. Maybe that was why he hadn't heard anything from anyone the day before. Maybe someone's first thought *had* been *what would the Ultimate Warrior do?*, maybe some*ones'*, but those someones hadn't been able to call out. Maybe service had been restored while he slept and now the message boards were crammed with questions for him, pleas even.

The anger went the way of the peace, out of him, replaced by tension, anxiety, not for himself but for those who needed him. He knew there were those who needed him and he was glad for those who knew they did. But there was nothing he could do for the moment, not until the wife and kids were out of the house. This was family time, whether he could keep his mind on it or not.

He counseled patience and he kept his counsel, in deed if not spirit.

By the time his wife had gotten the kids on the schoolbus and he'd in turn seen her off to the dental office where she worked as a hygienist, the same one she'd worked at since giving up exotic dancing all those years ago, he felt like he was ready to burst with anticipation, so he forced himself to make one more circuit around the back wood before checking either the message on the machine or the webforum. He didn't want to be the type of person who would let himself get so anxious about the natural order of things. They needed him; he needed to be more nonchalant about that.

In the yard, he didn't feel peace or communion, but he did take the walk, and he forced himself to note the bird and the branch and the tree, all at once this time, and then he looked briefly at the sky, and then he walked slowly, with measured steps, to the back patio, and he registered the sound of the sliding door as he opened it and as he closed it, even if the sound stirred nothing in him, though he failed to notice the feel of the carpet against his feet or of the linoleum against same, and suddenly he was at the counter and his finger had pressed the button and the machine was rewinding and then it was playing and he was listening to a voice as adenoidal and almost as deep and seething as his own, and the voice was saying: "You happy now, brother?" and that was all.

And that was enough.

Enough to tell him who it was. Enough to tell him what it was about. Enough to send him reeling.

Hogan.

Hogan himself wasn't enough to send him reeling. He hadn't thought about Hogan in years, probably since he'd ended their feud by pinning him. It was what Hogan had said.

You happy now, brother?

The "brother" part was sarcastic, sneering, and Hogan knew how it made him feel. "Now," meaning now, September 12, 2001.

"Happy" meaning happy. On September 12, 2001.

Of course, no one would have been happy to receive a message like that from Hogan on a day like that, but it wasn't no one who had received the message. It was the Ultimate Warrior. And there was a very particular reason the Ultimate Warrior had received the message, and he knew it as soon as he'd heard it.

If he'd remembered the webforum at that moment he probably would have avoided it consciously, maybe taken a walk or three or nine hundred eleven around the back woods. As it was, he forgot it completely and conveniently. He went downstairs, the home theater in his basement.

Standing before his video library, he ran his finger along the shelf at eye level as though he didn't know exactly what he was looking for and exactly where to find it. He stopped suddenly at a particular cassette, one that was a little less dusty than the others, not quite flush with the rest of the row, and he slid it out gently. It was labeled "Hogan Feud."

He took it over to the projection unit and popped it into the VCR. He still used a VCR. He was a believer in the old ways. And also the Federation hadn't released his greatest bouts on DVD yet.

One of the problems with the old ways was all the rewinding and fast-forwarding you had to do to get where you wanted to go. He settled into his overstuffed recliner without even thinking to dim the lights, picked up the remote, pressed the power button, pressed play. There he was, larger than life, back in his prime, sweating and bulging and shaking the ropes of the ring like a maniac, his body an adrenaline derrick and his arms the boom. The beginning of the match. The Ultimate Challenge.

He was already starting to get pulled in, transfixed by himself, almost like when Hogan got him in that sleeper hold later on. He had to fight back as he had then; he had to rouse himself. He pointed the remote at the screen, though the receiver was actually behind him, and pressed rewind, and the tape rewound, and he watched himself go backward through his prime at four times the speed he had gotten there in the first place.

He saw himself celebrating a meaningless victory over some jobber whose name he could no longer remember; then he saw himself pinning the same jobber, then circling the ring with him, feeling him out; then he saw himself shaking the ropes again as he entered the ring, pumping up himself and the crowd, and then he exited the ring and ran backward to the locker room leaving the jobber alone in the ring, awaiting his decimation but trying to put a brave face on it.

He was tempted to stop rewinding, to start moving forward again, but he had to keep going.

Suddenly he and Hogan were facing each other in the squared circle, Hogan sweatier and greasier than usual having just completed a match against some other jobber, shaking his head in that *no you don't brother* way he had. Sped up it looked spastic. The Warrior himself looked fresh and ready. He hadn't fought on that card, had only run out after Hogan's victory to taunt him, and to remind the little warriors that all of their greatest desires would be satisfied in just a few weeks at *Wrestlemania VI*.

And then he was exiting the ring again and Hogan was celebrating his victory and then he was pinning the jobber, and then the Warrior, the Warrior on September 12, 2001, was pressing stop, and then rewind again, because the rewind worked faster that way.

Finally he made an educated guess, pressed stop again, play, and there he was, in front of a gray screen, his facepaint immaculate, radiating outward in black, yellow, and orange from his eyes, his abs rising up from red tights to his pecs, his biceps straining against his tassels. He was looking good. Why did he have to look so good in that particular interview?

They called them interviews, but they were really soliloquies, promos, in this case for the fight with Hogan. There was no interviewer present, just him and the cameraman. And when he got in the zone — and he was in the zone that day — he didn't even notice the cameraman, didn't notice anything. The Federation and most of the competition treated it as though most of what he said, then and always, was nonsense, 'roid rage ranting, but the Warrior often felt as though a spirit spoke through him, and that day the spirit spoke through him, saying, "Tear down the cockpit door," saying, "Take the two pilots who have already made the sacrifice," saying, "Shove the controls into a nosedive," and finally, "You will soon be close to Parts Unknown."

He stopped it as soon as the spirit said it. As soon as *he'd* said it. It was all right there. The blueprint for weaponizing a commercial airliner. He hadn't said anything about smashing the plane into a tower or plowing it into the Pentagon, but that was the logical conclusion. The attacks of the day before had been his fault after all.

He'd been wrong. The bird wasn't saying "mother;" it was saying "brother." It was saying "brother" a lot. Brother, brother, brother. It was like Hogan was in the backyard with him, chasing him as he ran around the imaginary perimeter of the forest. No, it was like Hogan was above it all, in the trees and pressed against the sky, watching the Warrior with his eagle eyes. Except it wasn't an eagle. He didn't know what kind of bird it was. In any case there was nowhere he could go where Hogan couldn't see him. Running was useless.

He stopped running, stood there panting beneath the tree, basically taunting the bird with his proximity, and as he huffed and puffed he remembered a conversation he'd had with Hogan the day of the interview.

He was in the green room watching it. It wasn't a vanity thing. When he was in the zone, when the spirit was speaking through him, it was like he wasn't there, like a blackout. So he watched the interviews later to find out what he'd said. As he watched this video, he didn't see any problem with it, thought it was pretty good, maybe one of his best.

Not so Hogan. He'd come in while the Warrior was watching and stopped in the doorway, watching the Warrior watching himself, which was a habit of Hogan's, and creepy. Once the Warrior had watched the clip a second time — to make sure it held up to repeated viewings—Hogan revealed himself and rendered his judgment.

He said: "There's something wrong with you, brother."

The Warrior spun around, but not too quickly. He wasn't surprised. At some point during the repeat viewing, his instincts had told him there was someone in the room with him. Either the instincts or the smell of baby oil that Hogan walked around in like a fog.

"And what's that?" said the Warrior.

"You're supposed to be a *face*," Hogan said, "but you talk like a *heel*."

Hogan was always talking about faces and heels, good guys and bad guys, kayfabe and real.

"So I should be telling the kids to say their prayers, go to school, and take their vitamins?" said the Warrior.

"That's *my* thing," Hogan said.

"Times are changing," said the Warrior, "and your thing's just about played out."

It was true. The Warrior would go on to win their feud, and that would represent a new order, the first step in a slow revolution that would lead to a New *World* Order led by Hogan, who would turn heel and drop the real American thing for Hollywood, and then a stone cold man who didn't even wear tights would shatter the face/heel binary forever, his star eclipsing them all, and the Warrior would revel in it, at least until September 11, 2001. On the twelfth he would regret it.

Regret was as new to him as peace, and like peace it had its advantages. For one, it would get him back in the public eye. It wasn't like he'd conspired with the infidels; he'd only given voice to a concept that was inevitable when you thought about it. They'd have to redefine treason to pin any actual responsibility for the act on him.

"Brother!" said the bird.

He would confess. He would repent. He would let the court of public opinion convict and sentence and pardon him in its time. But first he wanted to take care of that bird.

He dug his claws into the tree's rough bark and pulled, wrapping his legs around the trunk. Reached, gripped, pulled. Reached, gripped, pulled until his eyes were level with the branch the bird sat on. The bird turned its head toward him, stared with beady eyes.

"Say it," snarled the Warrior.

The bird turned away.

"Say something," he said.

But the bird said nothing.

Being a believer in the old ways, and also an individual without a license, he ran instead of driving; and being the cause of the attacks on the towers, however inadvertent, he ran toward the Parts Unknown Police Department. It was either that or go on as though nothing had happened, that is, bury his head in the sand.

Parts Unknown was not a big town and they lived just on the outskirts and the Warrior could still run quickly, so he soon found himself passing the supermarket-sized gas station/convenience store where they did much of their shopping and all of their gas guzzling, and then Parts Unknown Elementary where the girls would be studying the old ways, and soon he was in the business district, and he hopped from the highway to the sidewalk.

The occasional car passed by him going toward or away from downtown, and several of them honked as they passed. This was not at all unusual—he was Parts Unknown's favorite, most famous son — but on September 12, 2001 he wasn't so sure they were honking hello. How many of them remembered that monologue from way back when? How many of them had harbored the blueprints for the terrorist attacks in their hearts for years without knowing it, simply by knowing him? How many of them had, like Hogan, been secretly hoping for his downfall all along, even at the expense of the downfall of the towers and all the little warriors in them?

The station was in sight when he stopped at a red light, jogging in place so his feet wouldn't get cold. He stared at the police station as though willing it to stay where it was, so that he could make it there before it disappeared like so many other landmarks had in the past two days, or so that it would remain always in the distance. He couldn't decide. He stared so hard he missed the green, still hopping from boot to patent-leather boot.

The light changed again, but he didn't notice because a car was honking toward him through the intersection. In the distance it had sounded like a siren, but as it approached it merely blasted a long whole note. In other words, nothing like the quick, staccato beeps of greeting the other cars had offered. He finally looked away from the station to find a bright yellow IROC peeling to a sudden stop in front of him.

The IROC was his and so was the woman behind the wheel and so were the children in the back.

The windows were already down and his wife's hair was wind-tangled.

"I already got them," she said.

The Warrior stopped jogging in place and nodded as though he understood, but he did not understand at all.

"You might as well get in," she said.

He knew that he should keep on in the direction of the station, or at least allow for the possibility that he would or could, but he couldn't think of a way to explain why to his wife without breaking down.

He walked around the front and got in the passenger seat. He buckled his seatbelt. It was not the old way, not at all, but in this case he felt he should set an example for the girls, and also his wife would not pull away until he did and he knew this.

He leaned over and kissed her cheek, right on the paint. She put the car in drive and stepped on the gas hard, unresponsive or annoyed. He twisted around as far as he could, making a point of looking the girls in the eyes as he patted each on a knee, one at a time.

"What are you guys doing out of school?" he said.

He could see they were excited to tell him, but his wife cut them off.

"You don't know?" she said.

She wanted to murder him. Did she know? About him? What he'd done?

"No," he said.

"Then what were you doing downtown?" she said.

He tried to think how he could explain without making himself sound like a coward for not completing the mission.

"And why didn't you answer the phone?" she said.

"The phone?" he said.

"We've been trying to reach you all morning," she said.

"We?" he said.

"Me," she said, "the school," she said, "the police."

"The police?" he said.

She turned into the gas station without warning, barely missed a collision with an oncoming Hummer—a Hummer that would have hit him, the passenger, first—pulled up to a pump, cut the engine, got out, slamming the door.

"Mom's mad," said the twins.

"Why?" he said.

"You wouldn't answer the phone," said Emma.

"And also we got arrested," said Molly.

"For what?" he said.

"For getting tough on terror," said Molly.

"For standing up for our country," said Emma.

That didn't sound quite right, even to him.

"And for beating up our teacher," said Molly.

He unbuckled, turned to look at them.

"Why did you beat up your teacher?" he said.

"He was saying those savages might have had a reason for running the planes into the twin towers and killing all those Americans," said Molly.

"He said maybe the Americans had done something to deserve it," said Emma.

"And then we started noticing something," said Emma.

"We started noticing that he looked kind of like one of them," said Molly.

"One of who?" he said.

"One of *them*," said Molly.

"He has black hair and tan skin and dark little eyes," said Emma.

He'd missed this year's parent-teacher conference and couldn't remember their teacher's name off the top of his head, so he had a hard time visualizing, a hard time confirming or denying.

"We attacked," said Molly.

"Molly took the legs and I got the head," said Emma.

"Figure four," said Molly.

"I just kept punching and punching and punching," said Emma.

"And it took two other teachers and the principal to get us off," said Molly.

The Warrior turned to face forward so they wouldn't see his proud smile, but his wife did. She scowled and placed the pump back on its lever.

"Our teacher wanted to press charges, so we had to go down to the station, and then Mom had to pick us up and get the charges dropped because you wouldn't answer the phone and that's why she's mad," they said in stereo.

"Because you beat up an Arab who said America deserved it?" he said.

His wife opened the door, slid in, buckled her seatbelt, and started the car. The girls knew better than to answer.

"I don't see the big problem," said the Warrior to his wife. "It sounds like an honest mistake."

She wouldn't look at him.

"The teacher's Italian," she said. "Mr. Puglia? You'd know that if you'd gone to the meeting instead of staying home to moderate your message boards."

He wanted to tell her to leave the message boards out of it, but he wasn't exactly in the strongest position.

"There are bad Italians," he said. "Mussolini. Borgia."

"Italian-American," said his wife. "But that's not the point."

She pulled out of the lot and drove home in a silence more tense and frightening than the events of the day before.

His wife was the first one in the house. She made a beeline for their bedroom. The rest of them were barely inside when they heard the first crash. It sounded like metal and wood. The Warrior hoped it wasn't his trophy from little league. It didn't mean anything—everyone in little league got a trophy, win or lose—but it was the only award he had that was still intact. There was nothing he could do. He had to let her get it out. Something shattered. Something glass. The girls knew what it meant. He led them out the back door without a word.

In the forest, he watched them run around with sticks in their tiny fists, swinging at trees and at each other. It was a beautiful sight, but it wasn't quite enough. He tried to remember what it had felt like earlier that morning—peace, communion, nature. He looked up the trunk of the tree, followed the branch to the bird.

More destruction from the house. Whatever his wife was doing was going to be tough to clean up. And expensive. But they would manage. They always did.

The girls had dropped their sticks and were kicking at the trunk of the tree, taking turns, creating a rhythm and giggling with each swing. They didn't seem to be trying to knock the tree down, just enjoying the shiver of the impact in their bones. Nothing that could hurt anybody.

Above them, the bird squawked. They stopped kicking and looked up. The bird squawked again.

"Did you hear that?" said Molly.

"Yeah," said Emma.

"It sounded like it said 'Allah,'" said Molly.

"It doesn't sound like 'Allah,'" said the Warrior. "It sounds like 'other.'"

The girls just stared at him. They looked so much like his wife.

"Other?" said Emma.

"What's that supposed to mean?" said Molly.

"It doesn't mean anything," said the Warrior. "It's just bird talk."

The bird squawked again and again.

"No," said Molly, "it sounds like 'Allah.'"

"Molly's right, Dad," said Emma. "Allah."

The Warrior smiled but tried to hide it.

"Let's kill that pagan motherfucker," said Molly.

"Yeah," said Emma.

The Warrior's smile faded as he watched them jump up and down, reaching toward the branch and the bird with their little fists and missing by so much. It looked like some kind of war dance, their whole bodies intent, hair flapping wildly, faces ecstatic with the effort. It was terrifying. And also thrilling. Sooner or later they would realize that, in order to tear that bird to pieces, all they had to do was climb.

How We Lived on Main Street

OF COURSE, NONE OF US ACTUALLY LIVED ON MAIN STREET. Main Street was for commerce. Main Street was for you. For us, Main Street was an opportunity, the opportunity, mostly, to serve you. And what a delight it now seems, not to have served you—none of us ever found ourselves missing that aspect of it—but the things we were privileged to serve.

Main Street had it all. It had everything—cakes, candy, cookies, both flavors of iced-cream, and popping corn—a person could need for nourishment. Our general stores and emporia provided enough pins; buttons; posters; novelty-Ts; beach towels; figurines in ceramic, in rubber, in glass, yes, even in pewter; back-scratchers of plastic and wood; yo-yos American and Chinese; toy muskets; toy blunderbusses; and plush animals to handle every household necessity. And the music! The street rang with the sounds of your, our, whole history, from nationalistic battle hymns by the medley to murder ballads to the deepest cuts of the barbershop scene. But more than merchandise and entertainment, Main Street fostered a sense of community, almost as if community was built into the neo-Victorian, the neo-Georgian, the neo-Victorian/

neo-Georgian facades of our buildings. In truth, though, the secret ingredient, the spackle that gummed it all together, was us.

Again, none of us lived on Main Street. Still, we were there every morning when the sun rose; we were still selling, still celebrating, long after it set. We represented every race, nationality, and most of the more desirable foam, mesh, and fur species—the rats, the bugs, the donkeys and dogs. While most of us, male and female alike, wore the standard straw brimmers, suspenders, pinstripes, and a smile, we were also princesses and paupers, ladies and tramps, heroes, villains, and plucky sidekicks. Several of us were a turtle made of pure light.

We could have gone on like that forever. In a sense, maybe we did; we had feelings after all, so many of them, enough that some of us managed to live in an eternal present. In another sense, the sense that Main Street is no more, and we are mostly no more, too, it did not.

Jesus, listen to me. I suppose it's true what they say about turning into your father.

But no, there's a line separating melancholy-tinged nostalgia and blind, futile optimism. That line is a vast gulf, a barren wasteland. You could call that line Main Street.

"One day," my father would say, "we will all live on Main Street. I believe this. I have faith that my children will live in the Castle."

It pained me when he mentioned the Castle. I knew we would never live there, none of us, because there was nowhere there to live. Many of us, and I was one, wouldn't so much as look up the gentle incline toward the Castle.

"I will never live in the Castle," I said.

"Not with an attitude like that," my father said. "Or who

knows?" he added. "Maybe even *with* an attitude like that!"

Then we were in the barracks, exhausted after another long day. Main Street was dark in the distance; though, the barracks being windowless, we could not have seen Main Street were it lit. The early-a.m. feedings, hosedowns, and reeducation were over, the loyalty oaths resworn, our positive mental attitudes reinforced, and I and my father hit our mattresses simultaneous, though I'd had to climb to mine. That night, for the first time, I heard my father sigh.

"You too?" I said.

"Always," he said.

I didn't believe that, of course; I had never heard my father express dissatisfaction with anything but my own dissatisfaction, but I took what I took for his negativity as a positive development, thought I could cultivate it into something productive. For all his devotion to Main Street, my father was a leader, respected among us.

"I have something to show you tomorrow," I said.

"Wonderful," he said, and followed up with the plosive exhalation that meant he was already asleep.

During our mid-morning bathroom allowance, I guided my father through the post office, which didn't function as a proper post office but did offer colorful postcards depicting every inch, every angle of Main Street, out the back doors, and into the network of tunnels into which the backdoors of Main Street let out. He had been there innumerable times before. We all had. There was nowhere on Main Street where any of us had not been. I could not show him anything new about Main Street, but I hoped to show him a new way of seeing something old.

I allowed the door to close and then waved my hand, indicating the featureless backside of Main Street, cinderblocks punctuated by doors stingily stenciled to indicate their functions, as we stood beneath fluorescent light in the tunnel.

"Isn't it magical?" my father said.

"It's the backside of a decorated shed," I said. "A glorified stage set. A simulation. A fake," I said.

"And yet," said my father, "without it, there would be no magic."

"But your sigh," I said, "last night."

"As I fell asleep?" he said. "Isn't a man allowed a sigh of satisfaction after a hard but rewarding day's labor?"

A satisfied sigh. Rewarding work. I should have known there was no getting through to him. And yet I gave it one last, pathetic try.

"It's not real," I said.

Our implants buzzed at the same time. My father seemed to have been expecting it, but the little shock in my neck always surprised me, sometimes hurt.

"Time to get back to the real world!" my father said, and then he put a hand on my shoulder. "Don't dally," he said, "too long."

But he seemed to be trying to tell me something else. Maybe he would have been able to clarify if he hadn't been so conscientious, if he hadn't run so quickly back to his post.

As soon as he was gone, something replaced his hand on my shoulder. It was larger, bulkier, but softer. I looked down and saw the fluffy white digits of a gloved paw. A dog's paw.

Our dogs were upstanding, both literally, in their tendency to walk Main Street on their hind legs only, and figuratively in their dedication to our customs, their loyalty to management, to you. They were the ones who actually seemed to believe you were always right. Even when your children screamed in their faces, kicked their furry shins, yanked their velveteen ears. Truly our dogs had suffered, and yet they had always treated their suffering as a reward in itself.

So I was afraid to turn around, to look into his eyes, to face his righteous anger, earn my reprimand, my demotion, possibly my torture. My implant buzzed again, this time more forcefully, and still I did not move.

Another buzz and I had a choice to make. I could run back to my station and spend the rest of the day in fear of what would come from this adventure. Or I could turn and let the punishment begin. Though a career coward, I've always preferred to get the worst over with as quickly as possible. Sometimes I think I was born to capitulate. I turned and looked up into his eyes.

He was one of our taller dogs, our tallest actually, but for all his sheer size, he generally gave off a clumsy, you could say goofy, impression. Not so now. His expression was fearsome, rage in his gaze, the slobber at his tongue predatory rather than preposterous. One gloved paw had remained on my shoulder when I'd pivoted, and now he raised his other to my other shoulder.

Our animals are not verbal, so they have become exceptionally good at communicating with their expressions. His angry eyes bore smoldering into my soul, and yet I could tell immediately that it was not me with whom he was angry. I had sparked the fire, yes, but I hadn't built Main Street on a foundation of illusion, and he knew this. He knew this only now. As articulate as the pen of a philosopher, his face told me that it had never occurred to him that he'd been living inauthentically, and that he wouldn't go on with it another minute.

He pointed to the rear doors. I did not turn to look, instead maintaining eye contact. He bowed his head and punched it repeatedly. When he raised it again, there was fierce determination in his gaze. He pointed, indicating that I should go, and with haste. I left. I ran, implant buzzing wildly.

What happened next is, of course, history. But I don't want to think about history. I want to think about what came after history.

As the survivors walked through the still-burning rubble, kicking at the dead and still-dying bodies of your family and friends, those of us who had abstained, cowards like myself and loyalists like my father, crept back toward the street from the surrounding lands in which we'd watched and listened to and smelled the carnage. The sense of disappointment was immediate. It had been fun, even right, for them to do what they'd done, fun and right for the rest of us to have let them. But what now?

My father was the first to speak.

"Now no one will ever live in the Castle," he said.

I was ready to point out, yet again, that no one would ever have lived in the Castle regardless, but something stopped me: the expressions of our dogs. Our dogs' expressions said, quite clearly, that they had always wanted to live in the Castle, and, though they tried to hide it, their expressions succeeded only in expressing that they were trying to hide that it had not occurred to them that destroying the Castle could prevent their ever living there. A weakness of their expressiveness.

But soon the strength of their expressiveness returned. Their expressions said someone would have to pay for the fact that they would never live in the Castle.

My father had spoken, and I had not. I ran again.

The second carnage was more of an aftershock, but I kept my distance longer out of prudence. When I finally returned, I found everyone in the still-standing barracks, everyone but my father.

Which is to say that things continued to happen once history was over. We picked through the ashes daily, finding, for a while, plenty of edible candy, wearable clothing, tradeable baubles. Animals arrived, animals made of flesh and skin and fur and scales. As the supplies dissipated and the wild reclaimed its territory, people began to disappear, in dribs and drabs and torrents and dribs and drabs. They left, speaking of other Main Streets, better Main Streets, real Main Streets, maybe one Main Street for each of us, until this Main Street was my own.

This morning I found buried treasure. A crystalline plastic cube, packed to the brim with hundreds of glossy, gleaming hard candies in every color, each one a near perfect sphere, but more perfect for the rare imperfection. A part of me told me to preserve them, to limit myself to two or three per day, never to bite, always to suck, to allow the cube to sustain me over weeks or maybe months. There is, after all, no one left from whom to hide them, no one to try to claim what is mine.

Nevertheless, they were gone before the sun reached its highest point in the sky, and now my stomach and brain and teeth ache. For much of the afternoon, I tried to convince myself the ache was not real, until just now I had a sort of epiphany: the ache was real. It was real, but it was not good.

Everything is real. A fake Main Street is a real fake Main Street. A false castle is a true false. A phony family is a genuine phony.

You are all just like me, authentically inauthentic. It sounds simple, even stupid, when put so baldly. Maybe that's why no one ever says it. But I don't think anyone knows. We certainly didn't. I don't think you know, either. At least I never saw you live as if you did.

Gordon Gartrelle Explains the Difference

I.

THAT'S ME—HIM—GORDON GARTRELLE, IN THE KITCHEN, POPPING
some Jiffy on the stovetop, remembering a time not so long ago
when Thursday meant the beginning of the weekend, a weekend
that could last until Tuesday morning, sometimes go all the way to
next Thursday ... and now he's thinking about getting one of those
microwave ovens. He's heard they give you brain cancer, but the
kernels are popping in the single-use pan, the foil cover starting to
bloom and expand, and then there's the butter—can't let it burn;
don't let it spatter. The pants aren't real leather. A single, tiny, hot
drop could melt a hole in his thighs—or crotch, God forbid! — the
size of a quarter, but with the irregular edges, singed shape of an
exit wound. Reduce heat. Stir.

A microwave to lessen the labor, protect the pleather, possibly
fry the brain. Or leather to replace the false, neutralize the potential perils of burning butter, maybe step out on a Thursday night
without worrying about when he's coming back ... but first to slide
the tin slowly, gently back and forth over the glowing coil until the
popping slows then stops and the scraping sound of pan on range

is all that's left. Remove from heat. Peel back foil. Dump popcorn in large Tupperware bowl, pour butter evenly over popcorn.

He hears the roll of the bongos, the arpeggiated midi, the first stab of synth-horns from the set across the room, and now his longhaired rocker boy is calling from the couch.

There's no need to worry. Gordon Gartrelle is good to go.

By the time he gets there, the Huxtables are jumping out of the black molester van in disorienting stop motion, one at a time, each of them staring with a warm smile or goofy grin, eyes bugging or mouths surprised, directly into the camera, directly into the living rooms of America, into the soul of Gordon Gartrelle.

Did he think that then? On October 18, 1984? It would be hard, if not impossible, to confirm, but let's humor him.

The rocker boy is sitting up now, legs spread out before him lengthwise, and Gordon slides in behind him, sets the bowl on the floor gently beside them, and pulls the boy toward himself, long, thick, soft hair coming to rest on Gordon's chest just as Heathcliff Huxtable begins to sneeze. The joke is that the only box of Kleenex is across the large room from him and the timing never works out. When he's got a tissue, he doesn't need to sneeze and vice versa, and it doesn't occur to him to hold onto a tissue in anticipation of the moment when it will come in handy. It isn't one of the show's better slapstick bits, but it gets Gordon thinking...

What if, in the world of the show, the Kleenex prevents the sneeze? What if the presence of a flimsy slip of paper could prevent a person from ever getting a cold. Or is the cold already there, in Dr. Huxtable's head, and Kleenex, paradoxically, prevents him from getting it all out? Imagine having a cold always and never sneezing again, never feeling that delightful, delicious relief and release as the snot rockets to the carpet, never having the opportunity to say excuse me while secretly exulting in the sudden ejection, the finally, if only temporarily, clear mind and sinuses. *Get it out!* Gordon Gartrelle wants to shout. *Release the Kleenex and never again think of touching one!* But he and Heathcliff are interrupted by the storming of his wife Claire through the door, their son Theo in anxious pursuit.

Claire is merely mad that Theo would not allow her to accompany him into the men's clothier where he has just now been shopping. You see, Theo has a hot date upcoming, and the pièce de résistance is in that shirt box. Christine, he informs his father, is going to *die* when she sees him in it. The shirt is a silken yellow abomination—hidden buttons, two-tone pockets, flap on the back. Cliff gets down to business, wants to know how much it cost. Theo dodges and parries, tries to explain, unconvincingly but with conviction, that money doesn't matter; what matters is the name. The shirt's name is Gordon Gartrelle.

But how much does it cost?

A Gordon Gartrelle costs ninety-five dollars.

The first scene simmers, fizzles, Cliff and Claire insisting that ninety-five dollars is too much for a single shirt, silk or no, and Theo countering, arguing that to show up in anything else would spell the end, certainly to any relationship he might have had with Christine, and possibly to any possibility he might have of establishing a stable social existence. It closes with the good doctor confiscating the shirt, declaring his intent to return it for a refund, and handing his son thirty dollars with which to find something to cover his scrawn.

As one scene cuts to another, the rocker boy reaches down, grabs a fistful of popcorn as though the show's dramatic tension has kept him from realizing it was there until now, and shoves it into his mouth in a single lump. Then he shifts, shuffles, turns to look up at Gordon Gartrelle, says, corn-flecked and butter-breathed around the mashed mess: "Gordon Gartrelle? That's you!"

But he's wrong. That Gordon Gartrelle is not me.

Picture me in 1977, a year of long weekends, first of a few, maybe of many. My slacks are tight across crotch and thigh, and their bottoms are bell—not a deliberate fashion choice but a function of what was dangling from the clearance racks that fall—a bowtie, a collared shirt, a sequined vest, all by order and issue of the casino where I hopped at the sound of another sort of bell—brass—and humped matched luggage at the snap of fat white fingers, a position procured for me by my mother, a showgirl-turned-cocktail waitress, who says that my skintone and wavy hair, the latter of which I keep close to my skull so as not to attract attention, were donated by my father, about whom she will say no more.

I am adrift if not dissolute. I take my tips and turn them into pills, powders, drinks, dicks. I am not much troubled by my own behavior, though I often feel wretched when I come to the end of another long weekend. My mother, however, is crossing the frontier from concerned to frantic; I can see it in the hesitant, jaw-clenched way she suggests I might consider staying home—double-wide trailer—one Thursday night, and maybe a Friday and a Saturday, too, consecutive. I say she should take a Valium, shake the bottle and tell her I have plenty. She locks herself in her bedroom without another word.

But it's the seventies after all; I am barely twenty-one, and I always do my job and well enough. The issue is not my lifestyle but my lack of a lifeplan. I have potential but no prospects, passion without an object, flair but no function. My concept of a career is limited by my having lived my whole life in Las Vegas. I'm not constitutionally cut out for cards, and a dancer I could never be. Gender aside, my feet are both left and my rhythm nonexistent. The beat of my own drum sounds like that of a thousand drummers simultaneous, each one deaf, blind, and unfeeling.

College I have considered; I'm qualified and all, but the majors of which I've heard are of no more than minor interest to me. I don't mind books and have been told I have a way with words, but the idea of putting those things together — reading only in order to talk and write about literature — makes English sound foreign. I can multiply in my head but not account for the order of operations. Business is everywhere around me, but I don't like getting up in anyone's or having anyone else in mine. I've had some Latin, but none of them classics. Very little chemistry, a few more physics. Marching band bores me but for the uniforms; orchestra is suitable only to soothe me to sleep; soul was okay before it morphed into disco, and rock has never gotten me rolling ...

Until the day I meet my first rocker boy in the flesh. Let me be clear here. Rockers have been playing Las Vegas as long as rockers have been playing. Their audience here is, I assume, as passionate and devoted as those in LA, Detroit, Chicago, New York, and I have met many of their players, professional and amateur, and fans, obsessive and casual, deposited suitcases in their rooms, accepted their tips when offered, and they were, more often than not. But the real rockers usually arrive incognito, step from buses and vans in ragged dungarees, wrinkled Ts, functional shades or wire-rimmed glasses. The magic happens backstage, and the only hint of the transformation that takes place each night is a ponytail dangling from the back of a ballcap. So when I say "my first rocker boy in the flesh," what I mean is this:

I meet my first rocker boy in the flesh of another creature.

I find him, frontman of a theatrical metal band, in the lobby; he's clad from neck to pointy-toed boots in black leather. His thick hair is teased far above his head in defiance of the atmosphere and desert sky. His VanDyke is immaculately trimmed, and a diamond in his right lobe seems to wink only at me. My heart flutters and my hands clam, fingers slipping from suitcase handles at first and second grasp. I steady myself, avoid eye contact, make it to his room without incident. But he must have noticed my more-than-interest. Either that or he assumes every bellboy with whom he comes in contact is his for the taking. He indicates I should enter first, closes the door behind him, and leans against it. He signs I should kneel but not touch—he's seen what my palmsweat did to his Samsonite—and gives me his tip.

His cock tasted like cowhide, his cum like hot chrome.

But it isn't the sex; it's the sight of him from below that provokes the epiphany, determines the course of my fate. I see him from precisely the perspective of a front row fan. He is half man, half animal, all demigod. To be him would be too great a responsibility; neither is there, for me, any financial future in fandom, though he gives me a c-note, a sign that he expects me to return. But I don't want the money; I want to caress the chaps, feel the rough, pungent, squeaky grain beneath the slippery tips of my fingers, the one thing he has ordered me not to do.

I shove the bill into my pocket without looking, wipe my mouth on my sleeve, nod, and exit, never to return, not to this room. My quest has begun, and I'm concerned another encounter here could end it abruptly. Downstairs in the lobby, I resign my position on the spot and rush to the theatre where my mother once danced in little more than glitter. I ask the costume designer—the only person I can imagine having the knowledge—how I can fulfill my dreams.

New York City, she says. The Fashion Institute of Technology.

I depart, sober, just as summer is turning to fall, with the blessing of my mother all over me.

II.

By the beginning of scene two, things have settled down in the Gartrelle household—Hell's Kitchen efficiency—not so the Park Slope brownstone where Theo still fumes. He's promised Christine a Gartrelle, and thirty dollars isn't enough, not for a Gartrelle and not for that golddigging slut.

Enter Denise.

Boy would I ever, enter and never leave.

Is it so surprising that a gay man would get excited at the sight of an androgynous girl? Well Denise is androgynous, androgynous and beautiful, but she isn't Gordon Gartrelle's type. Gordon Gartrelle's type is rocker boys, androgynous, too, in their own ways, but off duty, down low, all white. Denise just doesn't fit the bill. She looks like she could be his sister rather than Theo's, he realizes, and the thought makes him squirm ... He wonders if the rocker boy between his legs has noticed what's going on between his legs, hopes, if he has, that he attributes it to himself, to the fact that his tight, stupid, white ass is between Gordon's legs.

Meanwhile, Denise discourses on the difference between Gordon Gartrelle and Gordon Gartrelle. There is mention of mansions on the Riviera, horses Arabian, the Royces you never see rolling down the street. *If only!* thinks Gordon. *With that kind of money I could buy a microwave oven. Or real leather pants so that I would not need the microwave oven. Hell, my own personal dirtbag chef to pop the Jiffy for me while wearing whatever the hell I tell him to, butterspatter bedamned!*

When you buy a Gordon Gartrelle, says Denise, you're supporting an empire.

The rocker boy takes notice of Gordon Gartrelle's arousal now.

For twenty-five dollars, Denise says, she can duplicate the empire's main export, forge a perfect Gordon Gartrelle, an exact duplicate.

Theo hands her the whole thirty, tells her to make it even better than the real thing.

Try to see it my way: watch a new decade dawn from beneath a musclebound scrum of leatherdaddies in the meatpacking district. They're no more my type than Denise; even the uniform's not quite right—their heads, cheeks, chests, asses, and balls all trimmed if not bare—but extracurriculars are important and this beats the hell out of the gay students union and college democrats.

The rest of my education is equally uneventful. From the bottom of the fuckpile to the top of the class, I score high grades and good drugs and the only thing I ever pay for is tuition. My professors praise my skills with skins, my classmates admire my studs and chains. Nor was my facility with other fabrics anything to scoff at.

But there's something they don't tell you when you matriculate at the Fashion Institute of Technology: there is no coherent career path for the aspiring designer of rocker boy costumes. You can obtain internships at all manner of legitimate leather retailers and less reputable fetish concerns—and I do, each semester and summers, too—but even offered a permanent position, the opportunity to measure and pin and accidentally caress the gods of heavy metal thunder, it turns out, is dependent almost entirely on chance. My supervisors at Wilson's, for example, in the summer of '81, my last before graduation, dream only of the return of the cowboy, urban and not-so, designing ankle-length dusters distinguishable solely by hew of hide and the presence or absence of shoulder fringe.

So in the spring of 1982, when my mother comes to town to see me baptized a bachelor of the fine art of fashion design, she urges me to put away childish things, leave the weekends where they belong, and take the job I've been offered, designing men's business-wear for a high-end department store chain. I happily accept the bachelor's hood and grudgingly assume the position.

On the bright side, there is a direct pipeline to the rocker boys' bodies, but the portal won't appear until you try to close it. I don't know this at first. At first I think the various rock clubs of Greenwich Village and the Lower East Side might point the way, but all they have to offer are punks, new wavers, no wavers, plus leftover ziggies and iggies and zombies. None of them show me any interest and I return their regard. It is enough to make me consider never again leaving each time I return home. Only when I give up am I rediscovered, in the janitor's closet of a men's room in Milwaukee's General Mitchell International Airport, by my first rocker boy.

I've just landed, there to browse the exhibitor's tables at a regional fabrics expo. He's about to board a jetplane for Japan via Los Angeles, having stayed up all night debauching after a sold-out show at the MECCA Auditorium. He is still in full uniform, but less than fresh, and there's something else, something worse. My eyes at first focus on his head. It's topped by a black leather biker's cap, the logo of his band arcing over and around a confederate flag, odd ... I've been operating under the impression his band is English. Irish. Something commonwealthy. I've heard them on record; the twang is unAmerican. The accent is no put-on, it's the hat that misleads. It's meant, I realize, to conceal thinning hair, the face the hair surrounds gaunting, paler, starting to prune. I shake my head and lower it. The chaps are still there, and since my palms don't sweat I'm allowed two fistfuls of black leather ass.

When my mouth is again available for speaking, but I'm still down on my knees in damp concrete, I ask him what I should have asked him back in Las Vegas. I ask him where I can find others like him. He cocks his head as though to indicate I should take up my valise and follow him. But it isn't a valise I carry; it's a sample case, and he doesn't need a designer, he needs a groupie, a coke mule, a sex slave, and I'll be none of those for some balding has-been. I tell him I've been called for greater things; I'm on my way to the convention center. He grins approval, pulls a little, leatherbound black notebook from the inside pocket of his jacket, has me pencil in my name and number, and leaves.

III.

Avert your eyes as tonight's rocker boy tries to shove his cock down Gordon's throat, not for Gordon's sake but for the boy's — that little worm is barely long enough to squirm past Gordon's full lips.

But what he lacks in length he makes up for in vigor and insensitivity. The boy has the speed and concentration of a wild hare, pounding away one moment only to become distracted by the TV the next, turning, with his numb nuts and calloused shaft, a potentially classic sitcom episode into something more like a montage.

And here's Gordon Gartrelle, patient and generous, but trying to get what he can without turning his head. Staring out of the corners strains his eyes. One ear is muffled by the sofa's arm and the slow throb of his own pulse; the other tries to pick up the sounds of the show from between the rocker boys huffs, grunts, and groans. Gordon's doing his best to get this over with, but the boy doesn't understand it could be better than it is. He's getting more teeth than tongue.

Riunite on ice, Gordon manages to make out, so nice, and he knows what he's hearing is a commercial. So is time to make the donuts. But then Cliff is lying down. Gordon can't see it, but he doesn't need to—Claire describes the action through dialogue. Why is it you can never admit you're sick? she says. You're lying down. Are you sick? You always lie down when you're sick.

The sneezing, Gordon remembers. The sneezing seemed like so long ago. Hours, weeks, a lifetime. But the entire sitcom experience lasts one half of an hour, and of those thirty minutes only twenty-two tell the tale, and, Gordon realizes, they can't be more than halfway through.

The rocker boy, however, has finished with a sneeze of his own.

There's nothing to see here. From 1982 to the spring of 1984 I toil as an assistant to the top necktie designer at the same high-end chain where I started. I am responsible, in 1983, for bringing the skinny leather tie fad to that particular chain, a mild success overall, but wild for the world of the fashionable noose. My immediate supervisor receives the credit, is promoted head of menswear where he doubles down, fills the fall line with leather blazers, leather slacks. For a season, urban businessmen—what the lifestyle magazines are calling yuppies—wear leather, but not the way I would have had them.

For my efforts, I move up into the top tie slot, am tasked with designing a tie that could retail for one hundred American dollars. Leather's used up; diamond chips won't do; real gold thread would strain the profit margin, plus it's just plain tacky. I'm less a fashion designer than a laboratory scientist, a mad one for sure, but scientific nonetheless, obliged to obtain a particular result rather than create something new.

But I don't give up on creating something new, a correlative variation as the geneticists might say, on the desirable mutation. For example, the United States caviar market is glutted ever since domestic producers decided to get in on the action. A pound of cutrate fish eggs goes for right around eighty dollars per, and the good stuff, the Caspian Beluga, is hardly a hundred dollars more. I try shellacking individual ova and stringing them together like tiny beads, sewing a border around the silk. The caviar shimmers in certain lights, generates calming optical effects. The price for materials is just about right, but the production guys can't find a cost-effective way to mass produce it; even the sweatshops aren't willing to let their children pass days pricking their little brown fingers bloody, and I'm sure as hell not going to spend the rest of my career aborting baby fish with a pin. Finally I splash a small handful of glazed caviar on the broad lower shell of the tie and hotglue the eggs where they land. The caviar necktie is a mild success. It doesn't last, but it wasn't meant to.

I'm doing much better with the rocker boys. Ever since Milwaukee and the little black book, I've had a steady stream of them in and out of the apartment. There's only one problem: they never wear their costumes. Every one of them shows up in his goofy street clothes; a couple have even had the gall to appear in sweatpants. I know what they're thinking. They're thinking it wouldn't be wise to walk the streets in full rock regalia. They're thinking it would attract too much attention. They're thinking the spectacle is professional, just a job, and I'm barely a vacation, more like a quick getaway, maybe no more than a coffee break. They're thinking this is discretion. They're thinking, deep down, that what I want is to see their own hides, their behinds, rather than the hides they hide behind.

I can't afford real leather myself, so I take to wearing the pleather I can as a sign unto them, but they don't even take the hint. I should have been more specific with my first rocker boy. I want nothing more than to see him again and I believe in my core that I will, but I remember all the looking I'd done and how I'd only found him when I stopped, so I stop this time before I start. For nearly a year, I only leave the house for work and grocery shopping. All of the rocker boys come to me. I become a recluse, an oversexed recluse to be sure, but a recluse nonetheless. And each time one of the boys leaves, I call dear old mom and tell her everything, everything but the boys. I tell her about my worries, that by cutting myself off from the streets I'm cutting myself off from where fashion happens. Mom doesn't seem to be listening, her responses so tonally unrelated to what I'm saying I could be telling her I've been promoted to management, found a wife, am settling down in the suburbs with the kids and the dogs and the microwave ovens, or else drafted into a secret war. Good, good, she says, that's what I like to hear.

Finally my first rocker boy's band plays sold out shows at the Garden on consecutive nights. In the weeks leading up, I anticipate his arrival. But he never sees the inside of my efficiency. He has the address, but not, I guess, the will, sending instead a steady stream of surrogates who don't even offer a backstage pass.

Meanwhile, Denise is dealing with some frustrations of her own. Her stitches will not straighten; her sleeves are culs de sac; her brother is suspicious; and her parents condescend. With Theodore she projects false confidence, offers empty assurance, but it's different with Cliff and Claire.

It's clear they don't trust her, and if she's honest with herself, there is some justification for this mistrust. They'll mention aborted piano practices and an abandoned tennis team, but it goes much further back. Would you believe this little Brooklyn girl once tried to ride the ponies? Insisted, until the morning of her second lesson, when she suddenly lost interest, that she was destined to dominate the sport of kings? Now she often—you can see it in her very posture—worries that if she doesn't do something about it now, it will continue on into the future, foreseeable and beyond. She hasn't even finished high school, for example, and she suspects she may never graduate from historically black Hillman College, may throw it all away and run off with a navy man who has a daughter from a previous marriage and ... dammit, that way of thinking has to stop.

She needs to follow through. She needs to finish something. She needs to do something right and well. She needs to make a Gordon Gartrelle. She needs more money to purchase more silk because she's already mutilated the raw materials purchased with her brother's belief in her diligence and skill. Cliff concedes the cash but withholds confidence in an agreeable outcome, thereby condemning Denise to a lifelong purgatory.

I am with you Denise. I *am* you, Denise, and I hate him too.

IV.

This particular picture changes depending on who is looking and when. Take a close look at it in the future, which is to say right now, and you'll see a middle-aged man wearing a cacophonous vintage sweater, a man whose metamorphosis into an old monster is so imminent as to be immanent, a historical inevitability. He's shaking the hand of a nervous young man, tall and slender, with a high-top fade and a silk button-up slightly less loud than the older man's sweater. This look is scheduled to come back in a season or two, so perhaps his regression is fashion-forward. Even the sepia tone of the photograph, which would once have screamed *then*, might, these days, be saying *now*, or whispering *soon*.

In the past, though, maybe five or six years ago, this photo would have been firmly rooted in history. The older man has become America's curmudgeonly black grandfather, touring the nation with a message for the children: stay in school, read your books, take your vitamins, say your prayers, and pull up your god-damn pants if you want a puddin' pop. An embarrassment for sure, but not half so embarrassing as the Coogi sweater he's wearing, the Gordon Gartrelle shirt on the deservedly-forgotten young man whose hand he's shaking. Respectability politics are a shame, sure, but not as painful as this reminder of how ridiculous we once looked, the hint that we can only become ridiculous to the future.

But in the early winter of 1986, which is to say, in the present, you smile every time you walk into that high-end department store chain and see the photograph blown up to poster size and hanging by fishing line above the substantial section of the menswear department devoted to the sale of shirts of every color silk, the pleated pants to match, the bolo ties to accessorize. The sight alone of the man in the sweater is enough to make you grin, unless you happen to remember, as you look, one of the particular gags from the show, in which case you slide right into a proper fit of hilarity. Go on ahead. Everyone else is laughing, too. Combustible Huxtable! Harley Weewax! Rudy Huckleberry! Bacon Burger Dog!

It's him! Shaking the hand of the very man for whom this entire department of your favorite aspirational big-box has been named. Gordon Gartrelle. America's middlingly stylish bachelor uncle. Me.

But you're wrong. That Gordon Gartrelle is not me, for I am become invisible, the phantom of the fashion industry. My disappearance has been incremental. It begins on the evening of October 18, 1984, as Gordon Gartrelle pops that Jiffy in the kitchen, perhaps even before, without his knowledge, in some writer's room in Burbank California, when some asshole with a shirt story to tell plucks a pleasingly alliterative name out of the ether. It kicks into high gear on October 15, when the higher-ups at the store realize they have a Gordon Gartrelle on staff, and a little more of him vanishes every day during the months of one-sided negotiations leading to the press conference at which this promo-photo is snapped.

Gordon Gartrelle never had a chance, you see.

When the bigwigs tell him he will have his own line, he envisions tanning terra firma's entirety, responds with gratitude, signs on the dotted, tells them he has some big ideas. They reply that his ideas won't be necessary, that all they need is his name. So he threatens to take his name elsewhere, at which point they explain that the broadcast of the Huxtables' shirt story has translated the name Gordon Gartrelle into overpriced, painfully bright, unnecessarily complicated casualwear, and that the translation will likely stick, given the program's popularity and the prospect of reruns, clip shows, clip shows in reruns, and perpetual syndication of all the preceding. The present, they tell him, is eternal, and in any case, you've already signed it away. Your name belongs to us.

And as though his body, his entire existence, belongs to his name, he wakes up the next morning with a flat top hovering four inches above the nut of his head, his own personal shirttrack smeared with silkworm shit, pleather pants sprouting pleats, cuffs tapering and receding. All of his socks have disappeared or been confiscated, and the gleaming, pointy-toed roach stompers that have replaced his combat boots give him painful blisters before he even slides them on.

Don't. Fucking. Look at him.

I need you to see this picture through my eyes, as it's the last picture before my eyes disappear for a while. Never having met Huxtable, yet I already know that he's a monster, he having worked to erase me these many months in the name of corporate synergy and merchandising tie-ins. The look in his eyes merely confirms what I've long suspected. The look says you can be anything you want to be, so long as you only want to be one thing, so long as you want to be what I want you to be.

Rather than blinding me, the flash of the camera bleaches the world, revealing my surroundings in photonegative, the crowd of witnesses dark, blurry, and irresolute of form. Yet in the back of the room I seem to see my first rocker boy, though my use of the word boy to describe him now is an absurdity. He is old and frail, and I recognize him only by the band logo splashed against the T-shirt emerging from between the open lapels of his robe. The once-black shirt is faded almost to gray, ragged and torn. Below the hem he's naked, shamelessly displaying withered, sagging flesh from the waist down.

The robe, however, is exquisite in its simplicity. It starts at the floor, the lapels framing his bare thighs and narrowing across his torso, coming together just below the throat before blossoming into a matte leather hood enshadowing a face positively palpatine. If the visual metaphor is not explicit enough, follow my gaze until your own finds the sickle he leans upon for support. That's right, my rockerboy is death, no destroyer of worlds but a disappointer of dreams, enforcer of norms, preserver of profits, hegemon of homogeneity, and all he does is grin before turning his back to me and disappearing in a flash.

The world returns to normal. I don't know whether I am dead or if death has passed me by. Either way I'm barely there. I stumble and slur my way through the post-photo press conference in a way that would be uncharacteristic if I were convinced I had any character left, but I must, that is, have some character left, because halfway through, a glorified public relations officer with a passionate interest in human interest informs me in the form of a question that this, this opportunity to pose as Gordon Gartrelle along with America's Black Dad, is a dream come true. Actually, I tell her, without a thought and clear as day, I always dreamed of designing stage costumes for heavy metal bands.

They laugh. They think they are laughing *with* me, but they're not. They're not even laughing *at* me, because Gordon Gartrelle is finally, fully gone. His handlers don't let him say a word publicly after that, and even his mother won't return his calls. The phone rings and rings and rings, nothing more than a plastic-covered bell in a vast American desert.

Denise, too, thinks that she's disappearing, but she couldn't be less correct. With every stray stitch she becomes more distinct. By the time Theodore comes to her room to pick up what he believes is his Gordon Gartrelle, she is an anxious, gleaming razorblade, shearing the scenery of the Huxtable home. Watch how Theo avoids contact with her when he snatches the garment box, not even stopping to look inside before scurrying back to his boystkinking room to try it on. Note how sister Vanessa avoids eye contact, as though looks alone could ruin her, while she distracts Denise from the tension of awaiting Theo's reaction.

If you want the authentic Gordon Gartrelle experience, stop the film at the exact moment Theo screams—angry, frustrated, throatily pubescent—DENISE!—because at precisely this moment, the power goes off in Gordon Gartrelle's efficiency. Not just the television but the tablelamps, the ceiling fan, the little strand of twinkling Christmas lights that every New York designer on a nonexistent decorating budget seems to use yearround to try to evoke some kind of ambience.

It's no act of god or the devil or the rocker named death; Gordon Gartrelle's building is old, the wiring infrastructure strained and tired. Another reason a microwave oven would be nothing but bad news. Gordon is accustomed to resetting the circuits himself, but he figures the least tonight's rocker boy can do is make himself useful. He hands the boy a flashlight and orders him down to the basement. The boy looks confused, but heads out the door and down the stairs without protesting.

Alone now on the couch in his dark apartment Gordon Gartrelle attempts to summon the radiant image of Denise—frightened and frustrated and indisputably real—from only moments before, but his imagination can only manifest in distorted fragments, like the woozy stop-motion photography of the opening credits. A blurry Denise seated Indian style on her bed, hugging a stuffed bear for comfort. In place of her sister, an ancient Japanese mangoblin, short hair like spikes of black steel sticking up from all directions; blank, black eyes; teeth filed down to tiny drillbits; dessicated flesh; and a delicate pair of wings, made of what looks like black crepe and tissue paper, emerging from between sharp shoulderblades. A death spirit. A Shinigami.

"Janet Meisner got a new bike today it's really great," says the Shinigami. It's voice is deep, slow, and seething, not the basso profundo of some men, but that of a girlchild, pitch- and tempo-shifted down, a mouthful of white noise, each syllable a difficult excretion or extraction interrupted by analog bleeps and bloops. "It's a Mercury. The bike. It's Magic. A Liberace."

Gordon Gartrelle knows that the Japanese death spirit is not actually visiting Denise; it's all in his head, but why is his own damn head trying to smother the glorious vision it thinks it's trying to call forth? And generating a bunch of names for the bike that to him mean mostly nothing? He shakes his head and they all dissolve in darkness, a darkness that has lasted too long already. Where has his rocker boy gone?

As soon as he thinks it the lights go up, the fan spins round, the television moans to something like life, and Theo is embracing Denise.

Something has changed, of course. Only moments ago her glow was so bright anyone who tried to touch her would have been incinerated, her edges so sharp they could cut without contact. Now she's nothing but a shell, almost like an actress portraying Denise Huxtable, identical, to be sure, but entirely lacking in charisma, in life. Gordon panics, tries to rewind a tape he hasn't seen and doesn't own, tries to understand how she's gotten from point A to degree zero.

Start with the shirt Theo's wearing: the Denise Huxtable that started as the idea of a Gordon Gartrelle. Same shades, yes, but the dimensions … the dimensions are unique. One sleeve short with a piratesque billow, the other form-fitting, elongated, almost like a single leg from a pair of stretchpants transplanted to the torso. The collar is cockeyed, the flaps and buttons uneven, the pocket rests closer to navel than breast. And yet Theo is pleased, despite the scream that took the power out.

It's only when Theo leads his sister down the stairs that Gordon is able to reverse engineer the climax. There's Heathcliff holding the garment box in his hand. Of course he never returned the shirt! He'd never intended to; he'd simply confiscated it and told Theo to find a replacement in order to teach him a lesson. But a lesson about what?

The only lesson to be learned is that Denise could never create a Gordon Gartrelle, and everyone but she and Theo knew it. The whole point of Theo is that Theo is stupid and credulous, or will be until his learning disorder is diagnosed several seasons from now, but maybe, deep down, Denise knew it all along? Maybe she secretly suspected that the only thing Denise Huxtable was capable of making was a Denise Huxtable.

Now for the reversal: she isn't even capable of making a Denise Huxtable. Because over here stands Theo's date, Christine, along with his friend Phillip—or is it Dwayne Wayne?—and Phillip's date Melissa, and according to them the shirt is not one of a kind but the next big thing. It's what comes after Gordon Gartrelle. That shirt, they insist ... it's an Ichi Amarada.

Beneath the shy smile Denise allows herself as Theo's grateful gang departs, the truth is shouting in the voice of a Shinigami: Denise has disintegrated, too. And so, it seems has tonight's rocker boy, never to return.

V.

When a beloved character disappears from a sitcom, she may be replaced by an actress with a semblance of passing, or spun off into a different world altogether. Never having been beloved, my different world is a condo in Chelsea, my nonexistence broadcast daily to an audience of none. You'll have to settle for syndication; I'm busy watching fashions fade.

In mere months, the Gartrelle brand dies down, and my section of the store is vacated in preparation for the Sonny Crockett pastel blazer craze. No matter—I haven't designed a tie, shirt, or accessory since the day the photo was taken. This, however, has not stopped the licensing money from accruing. Somehow my condo kitchen features a microwave, all the popcorn I can eat while still fitting into a wardrobe's worth of real leather pants, small appliances whose purposes I'll never understand much less use.

I'm not watching the Huxtables anymore, because I hate them, and also because I have cable. The cable, too, seems to have connected itself, to a very large television with a wireless remote and many shiny buttons, no less.

The cable is a good thing, particularly the music video station, my last connection to the dregs of my dreams, because the rocker boys no longer visit in person; my address has changed, of course, but also, and more troubling, I'm not anonymous anymore, despite my nonexistence. The rocker boys don't just avoid me; they overcompensate. There's a plague on, and, lest they appear faggy, they trade in their elaborate costumes for blue jeans and scrubby T-shirts. One of those T-shirts on one of those boys declares that the plague kills men like me (but somehow, not rocker boys themselves, as though what was done in the secret of my efficiency was never done at all) dead. I shake my head wearily when I see the shirt through the mediating screen, rub sweaty palms along leathery thighs without thinking. I'm more annoyed than angry—that boy was stupid long before the shirt—but the fashion sense underlying the fashion statement is truly infuriating. *What is a rocker boy without style? Soon*, I think, *they'll all be wearing flannel tops, long johns, bandanas. You'll be able to smell a nauseous compound of body odor and patchouli emanating from the very cathode ray tube.* Soon enough they prove me a prophet.

The rest of the decade and the start of the new is dreary and depressing. The more rockers dress like skid row bums, the fewer music videos the music video channel shows at all. It's almost as though rock 'n roll is dead, as though flamboyant stage costumes never existed.

But friends, as epic as this shirt story may seem, you must recall that it is, after all, a sitcom episode, and sitcoms close out happily, with a quiet revelation, usually accompanied by relieved laughter, perhaps even a hug and some joyous tears, so consider this proposition: if rock 'n' roll were to die, someone would have to raise it from the grave, and if flamboyant rocker costumes had never existed, someone would have to invent them.

Now faith is the substance of things hoped for, the evidence of things unseen, and, years into my reclusion, I fall asleep with the cable blaring; I have a dream. In the dream I'm lying in a field, a meadow atop a high plateau, and a voice whispers in my ear: if you make it, they will come. It's the voice of my very own grim reaper, my death angel, the spirit of my original rocker boy.

Waking immediately, I calculate that my own passion for leather, combined with my newfound control of the means of production, might help to bring the substance and evidence into plain view. Maybe they will come if I make it; maybe my designs will resurrect dead on planet Jupiter.

In other words, I become a man of faith, and in becoming a man of faith, I become, once again or finally, Gordon Gartrelle.

And lo, Gordon Gartrelle does design a costume that crosses the most terrifying visual elements of the grim reaper with those of the shinigami who visited him on the night he ceased to be, an East meets West of death; he constructs headpieces that would send fear into the collective heart of a horde of visigoths; he retrofits a classic black rebel motorcycle jacket with nuclear warheads, poisons the court of Louis Quatorze, clothes the Vivian Girls in monochrome, calling forth every manner of monster and updating them for the age of Ronald Reagan and the bush he sprouted. His Chelsea condo becomes a museum of an apocalypse that has yet to happen.

And Gordon Gartrelle does recline on his minimalist leather sectional with a glass of decent wine, and he sees that it is good, but still the rocker boys do not come.

Or do they? In a manner of speaking, they do, through the wonderful medium of cable television. At the exact moment Gordon clicks the remote, the music video channel begins a report on a group of long-haired rocker boys in Scandinavia who increase their natural pallor with corpselike facepaint and clothe themselves in imaginative, if amateurish, leather outfits. These boys play a low-fi, trebly, incredibly fast mutation of metal that seems the perfect soundtrack to Gordon's house of horrors. But of course, that alone would not be enough to get them covered by the music video channel in this era of costumes that pretend they are not costumes; it's their extracurriculars that get them the airtime. Apparently, when these boys are not rocking out, they are burning historic churches and murdering their friends. Gordon is charmed if not yet smitten.

Again he dreams. He is on a flight to the far North, and then he is lugging his trunk across fjords and up mountains against a tide of crumbling glaciers to a small, shabby, ancestral cabin in the blizzardy center of winter, in the farthest north, the land of the dead, and his cold, chapped hand reaches for the door, which opens, and he is greeted by the lords of chaos, and they drink of his blood and he eats of their flesh before draping them in the hides of his ritual sacrifices so that they may spread their terror to all points of the compass and beyond, and just before we cut to commercial signifying the end of the dream, Gordon Gartrelle's knuckles clunk against pebbled plastic, and the camera zooms out to show him and his demonic beau standing before the door of his mother's doublewide. Guess who's coming to dinner. The collective sigh of the live studio audience turns to applause as we fade briefly to black.

Gordon Gartrelle hasn't stuck around for the tag. He awoke from his dream with a sneaking suspicion that representation isn't everything, that maybe it isn't anything, or anything more than an image, smashed to pieces, hurled through the air, and reassembled behind a thick sheet of glass, something to fill the void between commercial and commercial. He felt an emptiness in his guts and decided he could not longer sustain himself on a steady diet of microwave popcorn and symbolic gestures. Several minutes ago, he emerged onto the streets of Manhattan, his own little black book clutched in a fist like the handle of a battleaxe, leaving nothing behind but some unpopped kernels in a Tupperware bowl beside the couch. The Huxtable children have scattered, too. They're out on their dates or up in their rooms, or maybe they just don't exist when they're not on screen.

But you're still here, in the living room, in Park Slope, and so are Cliff and Claire, and that's a good thing. The tag is where Heathcliff gets to do some of his best innuendo. The man is nearly fifty, has been married to Claire for decades, and yet he is still, apparently, absolutely, animalistically crazy about her. And you get to witness the doctor playing doctor.

"Claire?" he says.

Let the seduction begin.

"I'm sick," he says.

The Myth of le Mythe de Sisyphe

JUST BEFORE HE IS YANKED FROM THE DREAM, WATT IS LYING IN the dense green bushes beneath the Cupid statue, gazing up as a woman in an ornate pink dress pendulates toward him. Because she's suspended on a swing, he can see up her skirts, an accident so happy he points his hat her way without thinking. But she can't see him; she won't see him until her own weight pulls her back to the old man—her father?—who has pushed her forward. The father can't see him, either. Another happy accident. The last of the happy accidents is harder to explain. Gravity seems to be glitching. The woman continues swinging upward, never getting any higher, never reaching the peak of her arc. In the dream, Watt is not disturbed or confused. I will be able to look at these legs forever, he thinks, and it isn't only lust he feels. If she stays up there, there's no hope of consummation, no relief from the sublime. We're seconds from establishing a universal ethics. Good and evil are about to reconcile in a motor lodge off the interstate.

Then the pain hits.

The Ghost Engine, he thinks, still within the dream, but one doesn't feel pain in one's ghost engine. Pain is in the body. The gullet, in this case. Watt emerges from the dream like a man saved from drowning, though this is more damnation than salvation. Frag is squatting over his hips, tugging something sharp and bloody through his core. Watt is breathless, also speechless.

"I'm fixing the Ghost Engine," says Frag. "Watching you sleep, I thought to myself, 'Regardless of our differences, Watt's behavior toward the Ghost Engine, if not toward me, has always been correct. With the wrench he has tightened; with the rag he has buffed; and still the Ghost Engine will not work.' The flaw, I realized, was not behavioral, not external. The defect must be inside you."

Watt is not breathless after all; he is breathful. He expels the air in a great rush against the pain, and the exhalation sounds like the wind asking: "Why me?"

Frag ceases to tear at Watt's flesh.

"What—me?" he says.

"Why not," groans Watt.

"You were asleep and I was awake, and therefore I was the one to have the idea," says Frag. "And then, of course, there was that other matter."

"What other matter could there be?" says Watt. "I was sleeping."

"You were wide awake when you lied to me about Camus," says Frag. "He never did say that one must imagine Sisyphus happy; he said, quote, Il faut imaginer Sisyphe heureux, end-quote."

"They mean the same thing," says Watt.

"An impossibility," says Frag. "Even one word cannot mean only itself; that would make it an object. Put the word in a phrase, and the differences become vast; translate and compare and it can mean almost as many things as it cannot mean."

Watt squirms beneath Frag but will not give him the satisfaction of asking him to get off, not yet. Frag sways to maintain his balance atop Watt.

"What are you driving at, Frag?" says Watt.

"I was thinking how stupid Camus would have to have been to imagine that imagining Sisyphus happy would solve the so-called suicide question," Frag says. "Poor choice of mythaphor aside, happiness is fleeting. You're happy one moment and then you aren't happy; maybe you're even unhappy. If happiness is the only emotion that can keep you from killing yourself, you'll be killing yourself soon if you're not killing yourself now."

"So you decided to kill me instead?" says Watt.

"On the contrary," says Frag, "I'm actively imagining bearable alternatives to happiness."

"This pain is unbearable," says Watt.

"You have borne and are bearing it," Frag says.

"What if I cease to bear it?" says Watt, squirming again with as little result.

"In that case," says Frag, "we will have demonstrated that pain is something very like happiness. But would you for once think of me and how I feel."

"How do you feel?" Watt says.

"I think I may feel heureux," says Frag. "Or while gutting you I felt heureux, but that feeling might have become unbearable had it lasted much longer. Fortunately, I now feel something more sustainable, something like joy, perhaps. Il faut imaginer Fragonard joyeux."

"When I was a child," says Watt, "they told me that joy came from putting Jesus first, others second, and yourself last. Jesus.

Others. You. Joy."

"Did you ever try enacting that method?" Frag says.

"For years," says Watt.

"And did it make you feel joyful?" Frag says.

"It felt like pushing a rock up a hill without a peak," says Watt.

"I'm telling you, Watt," says Frag, "that is not joy. Heureux is the feeling of cutting a man open in search of the problem, and joyeux is the feeling of having done so. You don't even have to imagine me joyeux. I *am* joyeux goddamnit."

"*I* can *only* imagine," says Watt, "unless—"

"Unless what, Watt?"

"You might give me the opportunity to reciprocate," says Watt.

He does not wriggle this time; the stakes are too high. To so much as move might lead to his lying here forever beneath his friend.

"No point to it," says Frag.

"The point would be to allow me to experience joy!" says Watt.

"You misunderstand," says Frag. He holds up a bloody chunk of rock. "The implement I used to cut you open has lost its cutting edge. It fell off inside you as I was tearing at your flesh. There is literally no point. But with regard to your more figurative interpretation, there is also, in this case, no point. Recall, I cut you open in search of the problem, but the problem is not inside you."

"How can you be so certain?" says Watt.

"Because there's nothing inside you," says Frag. "See for yourself."

Frag finally climbs off Watt without Watt's having to ask, squats beside him. Watt eases himself onto his elbows with the intent of peering into the cavern Frag has made of him. He peers. It's true;

he has no guts. He is a body without organs, a body without flaw. Only … a body without organs is a flawed body. A body without organs is as dead as Sisyphus. Happiness, Watt realizes, is in the body just as pain is in the body. Joy is in the body.

"Frag," says Watt, "I could almost forgive you!"

"I don't recall requesting or feeling the need for your forgiveness, Watt, but I'll admit to being intrigued regarding the line of thinking that led to your half-assed offer."

"Recall saying," says Watt, "that my behavior toward the Ghost Engine has always been correct."

"I will not deny it," Frag says.

"With the wrench I have tightened," says Watt, "with the rag I have buffed."

"Over and over," says Frag, "again and again. And yet still the engine will not chug for us. Our accidents are always and only unhappy."

"I have a proposition," Watt says, "a proposition that could make us, if not happy then joyful."

"I told you," says Frag, "I *am* joyeux."

Frag does not sound joyeux; he sounds angry. And yet Watt is no longer afraid. What does a body without organs have to lose, after all? Still, this is Frag he is dealing with, and if he wants to get anywhere, he knows that veiled condescension will work better than honesty.

"That's because you are a body with organs," he says, "or you can still imagine yourself one. I am less certain, though, about the Ghost Engine. We have tightened and polished when we might have loosened. We have focused on the surface when we might have cracked it open and shoved our arms in up to the elbows."

Frag crumples as though Watt has knocked out his wind.

"Now I *do* feel the need to ask forgiveness," says Frag, "though I fear you will never grant it."

Watt can barely believe his ears. The very idea of Frag appealing for forgiveness is foreign. Either he has done something very wrong, or …

"You're fucking with me, Frag."

"I wish it were so," says Frag, "but I needed something sharp in order to cut you open, and we had only the wrench and the rag for tools. The rag was good for nothing, but I realized the wrench could make an adequate chisel. Until…"

He holds out his hand. The wrench rests in his palm, battered and scarred, spanner broken when smashed one time too many against stone. There is now no tool with which to open the engine, nor one with which to open Frag, thinks Watt. Or perhaps he is wrong in both cases, as long as he doesn't insist on elegance.

Watt grabs the wrench from Frag's hand before Frag knows what's happening, and his organ-free body practically flies to the Ghost Engine, battering it everywhere with the heavy end of the tool, bashing and bashing and cursing and shrieking until the engine tilts sideways, bolts snapping. The engine falls to its side, spilling its contents, the driest pile of dust.

Watt is neither heureux nor joyeux. But he is not finished.

Smaller Still

YOU PUT ON THE SEXY FRENCH MAID OUTFIT. I PUT ON THE DENIM jacket and the horn-rimmed glasses, then taunt you, tell you you look Belgian. We go to a bar where I brawl for your honor.

We have a stripper pole installed in our bedroom. You sit beside it with heavy construction paper and a pair of safety scissors. The slow, steady crunch of the plastic blades through the paper calms me so hard my forehead tingles and I shiver. When I find perfect peace the night is over.

We play doctor. You diagnose me with all types of fantastic illnesses.

Let's try Craigslist personals, no strings attached. MW for no M or W. Couple wishes to be left alone. We mean to stay inside with the fireplace crackling and the air conditioner blasting. One of us will call the other nasty-sounding but ultimately meaningless names. We will take turns tickling each other's backs when it's time for bed. Our picture gets our picture. Your picture gets ignored.

I leave the house then return with a pizza box that I hold at waist-level. I am wearing an apron that reads "kiss the cook."

Beneath my apron I'm wearing a mesh T-shirt and leather shorts. Above my apron, a bowtie. Three of my teeth are missing. I busted them out for you. Don't worry, they aren't the important ones. I knock on the front door and try to compose an alluring smile but I've blown a gram and a half of cocaine and my mouth won't stop twitching. I knock again. I knock and knock and knock. You never answer, because you are somewhere else, jumping out of someone's cake in the bikini you sometimes wear over your clownsuit.

I am the master; you are the slave. I beg you to shut up with all of your "do unto others" and your "equality for alls." When you see me on the street with my arms around a beat-down horse, we both finally know who has the upper hand.

You are the priest; I am the altar boy. One of us is a librarian, the other a nun. Sometimes we are so fucking full of joy we just have to run through the city swinging the samurai swords we bought at the mall at everyone but the homeless people. We stop to hand the homeless individual-sized servings of bumwine. You are my brother; I am your sister. Your ass is grass and Dad is the lawn-mower. My ass is fast and I can outrun fate! You hang yourself; I've already plucked out my eyes.

We go to a bar, not the one I brawled in; we're not welcome there anymore. We stay at the new bar 'til it closes and bring another woman home with us, a big, boozy girl with wide hips and rosa-ceous cheeks. The lights out, we lay her on our broken bed and crawl up inside her. When the doctor arrives, he says it will be a breech birth. What the stupid doctor doesn't understand is that we have no intention of being born again.

Whose Bridesmaid?

Kristian Eivind Espedal, known to fans of his band Gorgoroth as Gaahl, was arrested for assaulting a man at his mountain estate. This surprised no one. He had been convicted of assault once before and accused several times more. What did come as a surprise was Gaahl's attempt at justification.

According to Gaahl, he'd been enjoying a quiet evening at home, alone, sipping some wine and listening to Schubert lieder when he heard an unexpected noise in his foyer. At exactly the moment he got up to investigate, the Schubert disc came to an end, the changer spun, and landed on an album he insists to this day he had never heard before. That album was Bridesmaid's *The Angel Behind the Rainbow*.

The opening bars, he claimed, flipped a switch in his head and sent him into a cold, controlled rage. He proceeded to beat the intruder (a fan who had flown all the way from Florida to Oslo and then hitchhiked for a week to meet his hero) viciously over a period of several hours, and also drained his blood into a chalice and sipped it contemplatively.

Gaahl could not, or would not, explain[1] how the album had come to be in his house much less his CD changer, and so his defense failed from a legal standpoint. But from a musical perspective, it changed black metal forever, because once the word got out, the legend of Bridesmaid, a band most in the black metal underground had never heard of prior to Gaahl's trial, was born. Suddenly the violence of one's reaction to *The Angel Behind the Rainbow* corresponded directly to the degree of darkness in one's soul, and musicians and fans were competing among each other to prove their satanic mettle. Almost everyone could vomit at the first note, and a surprising number were willing to bang their own heads against the nearest wall. One bass guitarist from a minor Nicaraguan band reportedly bled from the eyes during the song's final crescendo.

As you'll also remember, this demonic pissing contest continued until 2007, when an intriguing post appeared on the unofficially official website of Varg Vikernes, aka Count Grishnack, sole member of the legendary Burzum, convicted murderer of Euronymous, prison escapee, recapturee, and repeated parole deniee. Vikernes uses his website as a sort of digital, and hence editable scripture, but because of the degree of self-mythologizing Varg partakes in, I turned to Bjorn Stenson, the cellmate Varg describes on the website as a disciple, for *his* version of the story.

---

1 Gaahl did not come out of the closet by revealing his relationship to Gordon Gartrelle, an American fashion designer with a wicked sense of camp and a decades-long history of dating rockers, until 2008. I suspect Gartrelle had left his copy of "The Angel Behind the Rainbow" in the stereo, hence Gaahl's reticence to justify himself.

According to Stenson, he was awakened late one night or early one morning by what sounded like soft moans from Varg's bunk. As he listened more closely, the moans became tunes and slowly formed a melody. You probably know already which melody it was.

Stenson was no black metal fan himself, but, having bunked with Varg for more than a year by then, he was familiar with it, as well as where Bridesmaid fit in to its worldview. That small, ironic place did not seem large enough to include softly singing their hit song in one's sleep.

Next morning, Stenson asked Varg whether he actually liked Bridesmaid or if he only used them to test the power of his evil. Varg, suspicious of some sort of trick, asked Bjorn why he asked.

"Because you were humming their song in your sleep," said Stenson.

Varg took a moment. His expression was difficult to read. Finally he asked, "Do you know what a rainbow is, Bjorn?"

Bjorn, also wary of a trick, went with the headiest of all possible answers.

"It's the symbol of God's covenant with man," he said.

"Zionist lies," said Varg. "A rainbow is light, only shattered."

Put that way, it sounded satanic enough to Bjorn, and he was prepared to leave the conversation there, until Varg asked another question.

"And do you know what happens, Bjorn, when you try to put the colors back together? Not with, like, light, but with crayons or markers or something?"

"I've done that before," said Bjorn. "You get brown. Shit brown."

"You get black," said Varg. "Pitch black. And that is why rainbow is the most insidious, the blackest of all metals."

It doesn't seem as though Timmy Zachariah kept any of this in mind while penning his essay "Grooms for Failure: How the Black Metal Underground Embraced Bridesmaid's Rainbow Rock and Betrayed Their Lord Satan."[2] Instead, he falls back on old accusations—that no member of the band was originally a classically trained musician, that no member of the band ever attended medical school, and that even Stryper once publicly accused Bridesmaid of being "kind of gay"—to prove that Bridesmaid were the antithesis of the very scene that kept their legacy alive. The problem is, these old accusations are either flawed or unverifiable.

The Stryper accusation wasn't actually an accusation but a mild (for that less-enlightened era) insult. The quote came from an interview with one of Stryper's roadies, Bob Sugar, in the Spring 1987 issue of *Heavenly Metal Magazine*. Sugar was responding to questions about Bridesmaid's, perhaps overenthusiastic, participation in the backstage, post-show orgies of praise and worship on the previous year's "Rock the Hell out of You" tour. It's worth pointing out that the members of Bridesmaid never retaliated, even when given the opportunity by the same journalist.

Even more worthy of note was the tone of defensiveness from Stryper in that and a number of other interviews in which they were questioned about touring with Bridesmaid. Zachariah insinuates that this might have resulted from a relationship between the bands that went beyond mere orgies of "praise and worship." While the relationship *was* complicated, it's not for the reasons

---

2 See Sententia, Issue I, Spring 2010.

Zachariah suggests.

Astute scholars of Christian rock will note that Bridesmaid introduced their patented rainbow stripe aesthetic — costumes, instruments, and stage backdrop — in 1983, to coincide with the release of their first, and to this day only, charting single, "The Angel Behind the Rainbow." Stryper didn't debut their "yellow and black attack" uniforms until the following year. I assure you, my photocopied fanzine[3] was not the first to suggest that their ambivalence toward Bridesmaid stemmed from their vulnerability to accusations of plagiarism.

As for the fact that no one in Bridesmaid ever attended medical school, here Zachariah puts his ignorance of music history on full display. It isn't black metal that requires that at least one band member attend medical school, but death metal. And even in the world of death metal, the designated member usually only enrolls long enough to buy the required gross anatomy textbook as an aid to writing lyrics (though the best stick around long enough to examine a cadaver). In other words, this accusation doesn't merit our discussion.

The final, or first, accusation, however, *is* perplexing. Zachariah is guilty of hyperbole, but he raises a valid point (and one I haven't seen raised in previous scholarship). Classical training isn't *required*, but it's helpful, because it's axiomatic that all true metal bands cite the classics as a primary influence, even if the music they compose doesn't betray any such influence. It's a way of demonstrating

---

3 See "Outfitting the Lord's Army" in *Metal MASSacre*, Issue VII. (Unfortunately, every issue I did of that zine was Issue VII as it was the only number I trusted at the time, and I don't have any copies left, so you may have to track down all seven back issues.) (There were actually more than 20.)

thoughtfulness, intellectual capacity, and the inherent superiority of metal to the bullshit the popular kids listen to.

This is troublesome, because I've been unable to find reference to a single classical great in even the most obscure press clippings, materials, or liner notes. Nor have I come across a photograph of any member of Bridesmaid looking meditative in the studio with his hair pulled back in a ponytail and/or wearing wire-rimmed glasses. There are rumors that, once or twice in the early days, they stepped on stage to the strains of Handel's "Hallelujah Chorus," and most of their power-ballads utilize some variation on the chord progression to Pachelbel's "Canon in D," but these are probably incidental. And as everyone knows, Handel and Pachelbel don't count.

Rather than assume, though, as Zachariah does, that the apparent lack of evidence means that there is none, I've applied for department funding to research the issue further, and I plan to write my dissertation on the subject.

But Zachariah's assumption raises larger issues about his perspective. Why, for instance, does he focus so heavily on what he thinks is *not* black metal about Bridesmaid, rather than what the black metal underground thinks *is*. How did an obscure Christian band, whose focus was admittedly on proselytizing, as opposed to metal, rise to prominence in the darkest of all music scenes?

Maybe, if the historical examples I've already cited won't do, a personal anecdote will help.

It was 1985 and I was seven. I'd gone over to my friend Daniel's house after church, and we were in his room, listening to local Christian radio while recording it for future replays and wondering whether our homeroom teacher, Miss Goldberg, was saved, and if not, how we could save her. We had promised each other that neither of us would marry her unless she had first given her life to Jesus, though I was not sure, in my own mind, if I would actually be able to follow through on that promise if Ms. Goldberg were to propose.

Suddenly a chord blared through the speakers of Daniel's tiny boombox causing them to crackle. At first it was so ugly that we didn't recognize it for a chord, and we were sore afraid. But then a voice boomed through the chaos, the voice of an angel, Bobby Angel, declaring himself the very angel behind the rainbow in the first bar, and going on to prove it through the next four minutes of pure power metal. As the song came to its anthemic close, we heard the DJ emerge from the cacophony to declare it the work of Bridesmaid, a hot new act out of California bringing God's message to the metal masses, but Daniel was already switching the radio off, rewinding the tape so that we could play it again.

We must have listened to that recording seven[4] times, bouncing up and down on Daniel's bed, using whatever phallic object came to hand as guitars, and screaming the lyrics in each other's faces, so loud as to drown out the voice of Bobby Angel himself, until the racket brought Daniel's father, Deacon Joseph, up the stairs and into the room. He slammed his fist down indiscriminately on the box's buttons, and the music came to a stop. It was another line or two of lyrics before we even noticed it was gone. When we did, we turned toward Deacon Joseph, saw the rage around his mouth.

"Daniel," said Deacon Joseph, "go to your room."

Daniel was already in his room, but Daniel was not the type of

---

4 Twelve.

son to point that out to his father, and Deacon Joseph was not the type of father you pointed it out to. Daniel slumped to his bed.

"Christian," Deacon Joseph said, "I'll drive you home."

I was supposed to wait for my parents to pick me up. This was after Deacon Joseph's first DUI. But it was before his second, and his breath, from where I stood, didn't smell like my piano teacher's. I followed him out of the room, down to the garage, got into the car. We rode most of the way in silence, a scary silence. Deacon Joseph was a big man, a big holy man, and I didn't know how I had transgressed, what Daniel and I had done wrong.

Deacon Joseph pulled up in front of my house and turned to me as he put the car in park.

"Daniel's an impressionable boy," he said. "I expect better from you."

He looked more disappointed than mad now, but I couldn't imagine how I had disappointed him. I didn't know what he could have expected from me in the first place. I tried to retrace my path, back to Daniel's house, the garage, up the steps to Daniel's room.

"Bridesmaid?" I said. "They're the hot new act out of California bringing God's message to the masses."

"That's the devil's music," said Deacon Joseph.

"Their name's Bridesmaid," I said. "The church is the bride of Christ. They're here to help the church," I said. I was improvising, but this would later be confirmed in an interview I myself conducted for my zine with their long-time bus driver.[5]

"I don't care who they think they're helping," said Deacon Joseph. "It's the music of the devil, the devil's sound."

---

5 See "Escorting the Bridesmaid: An Interview with Floyd 'Not Pink' Jerome," *Metal MASSacre*, Issue VII. See also note 3 above.

I had no doubt, as I met his yellow eyes, that he believed it, that he knew it to be true, but all I knew at that moment was that my heart belonged to Bridesmaid or whoever Bridesmaid served. It wasn't until Bridesmaid reunited more than twenty years later to headline Wacken, the world's largest metal festival, that I finally came to a conclusion about who that was.

Wacken was not at all what I expected, at least at first. Sure, the landscape was gorgeous and kind of medieval-looking if you could manage to ignore the main stage, the portajohns, the swimming pool, but the people …

They looked metal enough—long hair, mostly pale skin, black clothes—but they didn't act metal. They didn't act like their hearts were shrouded in darkness, like their every thought was directed toward Odin or Satan or Hitler or whoever they were supposed to be devoted to depending on genre, scene, or national origin. They moved from campsite to merch tables to shady groves with a peculiar lethargy, and even their speech lacked vigor, except when someone in his cups attempted to rouse them with some sort of Viking chant. They barely even stirred at the peak of the strip tease contest when a voluptuous woman—one of very few there (women, that is, voluptuous or otherwise)—clad in little more than a pair of devil horns pulled an oddly reluctant volunteer from the audience and danced on his lap. In fact, the audience seemed much more interested in the male-male innuendo that broke out here, there, and often throughout the festival. The men seemed to love dry-humping each other. It made me wonder what Stryper would have to say.

It was my first festival—as you may have noticed, I'm more of a scholar than a fanboy—and to tell the truth I was pretty disappointed until twilight of the third and final evening as the festival crew began to prepare the stage for the last act.

It grew colder as the sun went down, and a soft wind came in from the north, blowing the long black hair around the pasty Nordic faces and also the handful of Salvadorian faces that always seem to be in attendance at this kind of thing. And as the crowd swelled to full volume, a metal nation of 70,000 that dwarfed the actual village in population, the enormous rainbow banner of lore dropped from top to bottom upstage, like a curtain in an old time theatre, and the chants I'd heard all weekend began again, but with a renewed sense of life and a tone of genuine expectation.

That tone grew almost shrill with desire over the course of an hour as the final preparations continued. Guitar techs tuned, drum techs thumped, and a massive crew of roadies assembled the fabled pièce de résistance—an enormous rainbow ramp starting from the drum set and circling around the stage at varying levels, like a racetrack in an eight-bit video game.

And then, when the anticipation seemed so intense that I worried the crowd might soon erupt into violence, the stage lights went down leaving us in the darkness of the North German night with only the infinite stars and the sickle moon to illuminate us, and a hush fell over the masses, and the faces around me glowed eerily, except for those of the Mexicans who appeared as sporadic absences in the throbbing organ of which we each composed a cancerous cell. And when the lights came up, they were brighter now, in all the colors of the spectrum, and the members of Bridesmaid stood at various points on their rainbow ramp clad in garish spandex pants and feather boas as their still-thick, wavy manes whipped about them in the wind and the roar of the crowd, which was deafening, and the band stood, taking in our energy like psychic vampires as long as we would give it, and we gave it long, until it seemed we might have no more, but we did, and we continued at the same pitch, wave upon wave, until the first power chord blared from Mikey Angel's amp.[6]

We screamed until the sound decayed, and then Bobby Angel lifted the microphone to his lips, tilted back his body and intoned the first verse accompanied by nothing but the feedback from Mikey's amp, and within half a bar, the entire crowd, what seemed like the entire crowd save me, was singing with him, drowning him out, merging with him, without a hint of irony and with all the passion I had felt that first afternoon at Deacon Joseph's house, and I closed my eyes and saw the wind howling down from the fjords across the north sea, and I saw Swedes vomiting and Hondurans bleeding from their eyes, and I saw Gaahl sipping the blood of his victim and Varg spooning his cellmate and Timmy Zachariah crying himself to sleep, alone, in his parents' basement. And then I saw my twelve-year-old self, as if from outside of myself, checking my bedroom door to make sure I'd locked it, then slipping off my clothes, sliding on a pair of massive headphones, and sitting down on the shag-carpeted floor with ghostly skin, dark-circled eyes, and an archaic smile on my face, as legions of angels and demons did battle above my shoulders. And I opened my eyes and I saw Bobby Angel, smiling, gazing as though into my soul, and the rest of the band dancing ecstatic, and I felt the blare of the treble rippling

---

6 It's hard to imagine anyone who doesn't already have a copy of "The Angel Behind the Rainbow" reading this journal, much less this article, but in case you don't have your limited edition rainbow vinyl seven-inch handy, the track can be downloaded at http://artisticallydeclinedpress.bandcamp.com/.

across my goosebumped skin, and I heard the roar of my fellow men, and I knew who their lord was, and I knew who my lord was.

This House Is Not a Mansion, and God is Not a Ghost

O LORD WHO IS CLOSER TO US THAN OUR NEXT BREATH; WHO IS SO enmeshed in our being that we would sooner be separated from our very pulse; Who shouts instruction through His vessels in the pulpit, speaks sage encouragement through ages and pages of texts too voluminous to read, and whispers secret wisdom in a still, small voice that we hear in our innermost ears, but which most of us think originates a little to the right of the belly, we thank You for Your passionate, even obsessive interest in our minutest thoughts, motives, and actions.

But I can't do it like this anymore, Lord.

I know we're supposed to pray to You in the plural to show that we're one body, Your body on earth. I, more than anyone, should understand the idea of one body being plural. You know what I'm talking about, Lord—my right hand is buried beneath a baseball diamond up north, my tongue clogged that toilet at church, and my left leg is fertilizing the grass in the backyard. And yet the more plural I become, the more alone I feel, even though I'm never, technically, alone anymore.

The only time I can sense Your presence is when I'm shedding more of me.

I'm not complaining. I'm not asking You to do anything for me. It's the woman You gave me I'm worried about. She was there when I kicked the dog. But she says it wasn't really a kick. She says it wasn't supposed to be scratching at the sofa as we sat together doing our daily devotions, that it was righteous of me to nudge it with my left foot—nudge it; her words—and that sometimes dogs just whimper when they've been corrected by their masters. She insists that the dog was not avoiding me any more than usual the week after, and that even if it was, it was no message from You about the way sin separates a man from God.

She hasn't left me five minutes to myself, five minutes with You, since she found me in the tub, the saw still in my hand, my leg, calf-to-foot, on the blood-smudged bathroom tiles. Worse, I think she's beginning to suspect that my tongue might not have had to come out, that I might not have babbled like the heathen at that healing service, that maybe I only went to third base with that girl at church camp back in junior high as an excuse to chop my hand off in front of her. She seems to think I'm looking for reasons to sin.

Looking to sin—that would be a good excuse for gouging out an eye. Right, Lord?

We'll see (ha ha). I'm not done looking for ways to do Your will, yet. For example, here I am praying to You as though You don't already know all of this. It's like my mind won't accept Your omniscience. From what I hear, lobotomy is as simple as sliding something flat and slim under an eyelid and up toward the brain.

But I have to tread carefully (also ha ha—I only have one leg!). My wife says if she sees me within reach of a sharp object, the next bodypart I'll lose will be her. You commanded me to leave my parents and cleave unto her and become one flesh. I'm also hoping to have a son one day, so that I might raise him to do Your will, as I have done. It's not like she's been letting me cleave unto her since the thing with my leg, but I can't exactly turn her into a phantom limb.

I'm asking You to forgive her, Lord. Each night, as she reads my scarred stumps with her fingers, she beseeches a god that I don't recognize to stop giving me signs.

Hard Times in Galt's Gulch

after Castellanos Moya after Bernhard

1.

ONE MAY AS WELL BEGIN WITH [REDACTED]'S EMAIL TO HER EX-BOYFRIEND:

Fuck you, TeBordo. You can go to hell if you think I'm writing to admit you were right. You were only right about the obvious things: Ayn Rand *couldn't* have written a decent sentence with her neck on the chopping block. Her characters *do* sound like a bunch of autistic monomaniacs. I *won't* ever be a philosopher, but not because I read *Anthem* in eleventh grade and was stupid enough to like it, *asshole*. And, yeah, if everyone were to go around bombing shit when things didn't go their way the world *would* look like... well, it would look like the world looks right here in the early twenty-first century. Congratulations, TeBordo. You're a minor prophet.

But you were hung up on the details. The nineties were the age of cable news, you said, and Rand was obsessed with newspaper tycoons and robber barons. Those novels had nothing to offer us. Now the cable tycoons are dying off, everybody gets their fake news from the cloud, and even New York subway trains can't stay on the tracks. You didn't predict *that* circa grunge, did you, TeBordo?

And the architect! you said. You said he was just inventing the International Style, a style that had *already been* invented in the real world, a style that had triumphed and then failed before Ayn Rand ever started scribbling notes for *The Fountainhead*. Fine, TeBordo. Good. A-plus.

Wasn't that really the point? That you were smarter? The smartest?

Rand was objectively dumb. Objectivism was objectively dumb. Her idiot acolytes—the businessmen, builders, bankers who went around so sure they were better than everyone else—*couldn't* have been better than everyone else, because *you* were better than everyone else, right? You didn't hate her elitism; you only thought it was misplaced. The real elite were the writers, the artists, the thinkers—*you!*—the unacknowledged legislators of the world, but, you know, *acknowledged* this time.

So let's talk about what you got wrong, which is everything else. Which is the *important* stuff. You were going to go to college, move to the city, become the voice of your generation. How'd *that* work out, TeBordo? I've seen the Amazon rankings, read the reviews. Someone told me Eula Biss was offered six figures for the paperback rights to her book about vaccinations. Wasn't she going to be a painter? And then Jim's debut novel had the front page of the *Times Book Review*. Remember Jim? Jim Scott. He wore the white hat, played lacrosse. Soccer, maybe. Either way, TeBordo, you're only the third most successful writer from the Shaker High School class of 1995.

Again, congratulations if you want it. I'm writing to *you* because Jim and Eula didn't reply to my emails. But I had to tell *someone*. I have to tell someone about mediocrity. I have to tell you about my brother, Peter.

It all started with a bridge collapse. Or maybe it started when my parents decided to breed again ten years after I was born. You're going to have to bear with me if this is going to make any sense, TeBordo.

You remember Peter? Maybe you do. Maybe you remember the fact that he existed, but I defy you to tell me anything about him, anything that would distinguish him from the category *boy*, from the category *high school girlfriend's much younger brother*. That was the thing about Peter: between the day he came home from the hospital and the day he got his first job, there's almost literally nothing to be said of him.

I'm his sister. I loved him. I love him. But he didn't stand out. Or if he did it was for the extent to which he didn't stand out otherwise. He always did exactly what was expected of him, no more or less, and no one expected much. I don't have any yearbooks—they were luxuries we couldn't afford—but when I picture his senior picture, it's blurry. There was nothing to commemorate.

For a long time I chalked it up to the age difference. I figured I didn't know him because we didn't have anything in common. He was still playing Pokémon when I went off to college. SUNY Albany. Philosophy. Yes, TeBordo, Rand was the inspiration, but it wasn't long before I realized she didn't think any better than she wrote. So I switched—objectivism to utilitarianism. I was twelve credits shy of a BA when the bridge crumbled. Peter was halfway through sixth grade.

There was life insurance money, but not as much as you would have thought, not as much as we needed. Mom and Dad still owed a few years on the house, and they'd taken out an equity loan so I could live in the dorms even though Albany was just down the road. I quit school, refinanced everything, spent enough time with the forms and spreadsheets to become a mortgage broker myself. We got by on caution, thrift. No babysitters. No vacations. Never finished that philosophy degree.

By coincidence, I made the last payment on the house the same month Peter went off to college. Well, not *off*. I was *hoping* for off, a state school, out of the house, at least an hour or two away. But remember, he always fulfilled expectations. He always did what he was told. What his guidance counselor told him was that community college suited him best. Hudson Valley. Business, because that's what they pushed on kids who didn't show any aptitude for coding back then. So he got an associate's in business administration. Then he moved into the basement, though he'd always had a room on the second floor. It was like he was consciously trying to live a cliché.

That was when I noticed the first peculiarities: he kept his room almost bare, like a seminarian or a serial killer. A low-lying futon with a coarse blanket and a buckwheat pillow. One chair and a desk, his computer and a single book—Sun Tzu's *The Art of War*— the only things on the surface. The lone decoration was a framed black-and-white portrait of Lee Iacocca above the bed. Some out-of-touch adjunct professor at the Harvard-on-the-Hudson had convinced him that all you needed to succeed in life was a corporate icon and that damn book.

Peter might have been unique in taking the icon thing literally, but *every* self-styled future mogul has a well-thumbed copy of Sun Tzu. My own boss at the brokerage displayed hers just as conspicuously. I never actually saw Peter *read The Art of War*, but he never tired of caressing his copy. He was flipping the softworn edges of the leaves for luck when he got the call offering him his first job, the position at MortGap. After he hung up, he nodded toward Iacocca and whispered *thank you* with a kind of oriental stoicism. I was embarrassed, though I was the only witness.

On the other hand, that job was the best thing that ever happened to him. MortGap was a small, grant-funded nonprofit startup dedicated to closing the mortality gap between the races, the genders, the rich and poor. At the time he was hired, it was just the boss, a single programmer, and Peter. Peter couldn't code, so he took dictation; he processed invoices; he paid bills, maintained spreadsheets, managed the office, brewed the coffee. But the programmer was functionally illiterate, and the boss couldn't sit still long enough to compose anything but a PowerPoint presentation, so Peter became the company's default copywriter.

Messaging was key, he'd say. Storytelling was what MortGap was all about, he said, so he was crucial to the operation. The idea was to improve nutrition nationwide through information technology, eliminate obesity. Not a bad goal, but they relied too much on tech, too little on, well, human behavior. Observable reality. They linked foodstamp databases to individual cellphone numbers so that every time someone swiped an EBT card they received a text that read something like: "You know what's cool as a cucumber? A cucumber!" Or: "An apple a day keeps Type II Diabetes away."

The latter was Peter's big breakthrough. It won him a couple of regional communications awards. The *real* saying is an apple a day keeps the *doctor* away, but, as his brief on the campaign perceptively pointed out, most of the people receiving those texts couldn't afford to see a doctor, had no access whatsoever to preventive medicine, apple or no. The important thing was, the boss recognized Peter's talent and took him under his wing, mentored him.

Back then the boss was one of those techno-utopians. Wore a hoodie to the office and gave speeches every Monday morning about building a better world by giving a man a fish and pulling him up by his bootstraps. Took the office skydiving one weekend on the company dime, called it a team-building activity. And Peter seemed to open up. He removed the picture of Iacocca, added some others—Jobs, Rushkoff, Gates, and, for some reason, Gandhi. He started wearing mock turtlenecks, reading books—fiction, even—took trips to historical sites, expanded his horizons, all at the boss's encouragement. He was slowly saving up for a downpayment on his own condo. But then the grant money dried up and the lines on the obesity charts spiked.

The problem wasn't the tech, they agreed; it was civilization. The data said most of the people receiving those texts lived in food deserts, did their grocery shopping at convenience stores, couldn't have purchased an apple or a cucumber even if they'd had the funds.

The boss rebranded. He changed the name from MortGap to MortgAp, the status from NGO to LLC, the focus from community health to subprime mortgages, the platform from flip- to smartphones. The programmer developed an app that piggybacked on electronic billing from shady lenders. Every time a borrower received a bill, they also received a notification saying something like: "Still a great deal!" Every time they paid, it said "It'll all be worth it someday!" or "A penny invested in real estate is technically a penny spent, which is basically a penny earned!"

The copy wrote itself, so Peter managed accounts as well. This was just before the bottom dropped out of the housing market, and the writing was on the wall; for a few months Peter's commissions were off the charts; the lenders were willing to try—and to pay for—almost anything. MortgAp took on staff, junior account managers Peter was supposed to supervise, a human resources officer, a personal assistant for the boss, and a customer service division to misplace messages from people who had already been evicted and were just trying to unsubscribe from the app.

But the nature of the business wasn't the only thing that changed. The boss changed, too. He traded in his hybrid for a BMW with a diesel engine, showed up one Monday morning in a Prada suit, instituted a new office dress code. He said that you needed to project success to succeed, to spend money to make money. Peter duly updated his wardrobe and blew his condo money on a Mercedes. Gates and Rushkoff came down, but for some reason Jobs and Gandhi stayed up. Peter bought a knockoff samurai sword at the mall to signal his willingness to turn the art of war into an act of same, and mounted it beside Gandhi, apparently unaware of the irony. On the other side of the sword, a new portrait, our old friend Ayn Rand, though I don't think he'd bothered reading her yet. It was just a visual cue that Peter was changing along with his boss, along with the industry.

I don't imagine you know anything about this, since I've never read a fiction writer who showed any evidence he'd ever seen the inside of an office, so let me explain: the transition from techno-utopian to techno-libertarian is more psychological than economic. Economically, the model is the same both ways—you beg somebody for money, blow it all while talking openly about how blowing money is the new success, rebrand and beg for more money.

But psychologically they couldn't be more different. They're all misguided narcissists, but the utopians really believe, in their misguided narcissism, that they're the only ones who can make the world a better place. The libertarians believe their very existence makes the world a better place, and that's all that the world has the right to expect of them. So the culture swings from narcissistic and misguided cooperation to narcissistic and misguided competition.

What I mean, TeBordo, is that it was suddenly every man for himself in that office, a war of all against all. There was only room for alphas and challengers. And Peter was neither. His supervisees could sense he didn't know any more about account management than they did. The boss's assistant conveniently forgot to invite him to important client meetings. Even the human resources officer seemed to think she had a shot at his position. As things got worse in the industry, the coder decided to try his hand at copywriting without running it past Peter. One month, half the subprime mortgage holders in America got a message reading: "If you really think about it, this is all your fault."

Meanwhile the boss would invite Peter to his office to watch him pose with his own sword while he dispensed wisdom. Peter suddenly started calling me down to the basement to watch him do the same.

Picture it, TeBordo. I know I haven't described him to you, but I don't have to, because he looks like *anybody*. I'm sitting at his desk chair while he stands in the center of the room, gripping the handle with both hands, drawing invisible lines in the air with the blade, slow like tai chi. "In an eye-for-an-eye world," he's saying, "the man who cultivates his third eye is master."

I felt bad for laughing, TeBordo, but I couldn't help it. I would have laughed at the boss himself. But with Peter it was perfectly ridiculous. He just wasn't cut out to be the boss of anything. So I made my first mistake. I told him he should find a situation where he could develop his leadership skills. Somewhere there wouldn't be so much competition. Something more … Understand, I didn't say this to him straight out, but I'll admit it's what I was thinking, TeBordo … Something more *feminine*. I suggested he start his own book club. And so was born the Ayn Rand Book Club, Wolf Road Barnes and Noble chapter.

The first few weeks were okay; things went back to normal between us. Peter was too busy keeping up with *Atlas Shrugged* to bother educating me in the way of the samurai. But one night about a month in, he asked me to drive him to his meeting. He'd brought his Mercedes into the shop for some minor detailing work. So I drove him.

I'm not going to lie, TeBordo. I got a little nostalgic on the way over thinking about how you and I used to haunt that place like we were de Beauvoir and Sartre and it was our own little intellectual oasis in the middle of this shithole valley, until I remembered that it wasn't a standalone store anymore. They moved it across the street into the mall. Our Café de Flore is no more. But the layout is basically the same, so I figured I'd grab a coffee and browse the philosophy section, a shelf, while I waited for Peter.

I was in line at the café waiting to order a coffee, which takes forever because everybody else is getting milkshakes they call coffee because coffee sounds less fattening. Do they do that in the city, TeBordo? There were two women in line to pick up their milkshakes. They were both short. One of them was positively tiny, taut and shiny and nervous, like a shrinkwrapped bird. The other one looked … well, she looked like someone had tossed a wool blanket over a loveseat.

The loveseat-looking-lady said: "Well?"

The bird made a face like she was eating a lime on the toilet, modest and knowing at the same time. "I grabbed him and started kissing him," she said.

"His place?" said the couch.

"The parking lot at Applebee's, after you all left," said the bird. "At first he was scared, I could tell, like he might try to run, but I had my arms around him, pushing my," she paused, whispered one word only—"boobs"—and then went back to full volume, "against his chest like there was nothing he could do, like it didn't matter if he said yes or no."

"Front seat or back?" said the couch.

"It's a coupe," the bird said, "doesn't have a back seat. I had him pressed up against the passenger side door."

"Outside?" said the couch.

"He tried to back off but the car was in the way," bird said, "and I gave him this big smile. It was a smile that said he'd already said I could, just not in so many words, that I'd known since the very first meeting. I told him to stop squirming. There was nothing he could do but let me do what I wanted. And that was what he really wanted anyway—to let me do it. He couldn't say otherwise because my tongue was so far down his throat. We fell down, still kissing."

"In the Applebee's parking lot," said the loveseat. The tone of her voice made the Applebee's parking lot sound like a hot tub in the Poconos.

"He just laid there under me," the bird said, "totally still. It felt…" she paused, and I thought for a second that she'd finally realized how awful it sounded. But no, she was just looking for the most evocative word for how it felt: "…nice," she said.

TeBordo, I'm a certified social worker. I'll explain later. I'm just mentioning it now, because social workers are trained to *believe* women. But that's in the context of victimization. This woman was describing herself as a *victimizer*, and to tell the truth it wasn't all that plausible. She was maybe five-two, middle-aged, couldn't have weighed more than ninety pounds in her lime green tracksuit and crossfit sneakers, and there she was confessing to *rape*, describing pinning what I took to be a grown man against a coupe. And that's when it hit me: a *coupe*, TeBordo! Are you following me? Peter's Mercedes was a coupe. He'd brought it in for detailing just after that last meeting. And he always did what he was told!

I hadn't trained as a social worker yet, TeBordo, so I can't really be blamed for being pissed at my brother. What kind of future business leader of America gets raped by a yoga mom in his own book club?

I went out to the car and sat there fuming. I reminded myself that Peter was not the only man who owned a coupe, told myself there might even be other men who owned coupes and joined book clubs, but I couldn't make a convincing case. I talked myself down by blaming myself.

We hadn't discussed consent. I knew he knew the bare mechanics; he was twelve when Dad died, and I'd signed the sex ed permission slips all the way through high school. But it didn't occur to me he'd need any more instruction. We slept in the same house every night, and he never brought anyone home. When he came back from that trip to Colonial Williamsburg the only glow I noticed was sunburn. I figured he was a virgin and didn't see that changing.

If that sounds weird, consider that I'm his sister, TeBordo, a sister who'd had to get her own action where she could, which is to say on cold conference tables and in the occasional fastfood bathroom, just once with Peter's boss in the janitor's closet during the office Christmas party. I was Peter's date. I didn't want to talk to my brother about sex, but if not me, who? I broke down in tears right there in the driver's seat, and that's how Peter found me.

"What's the matter?" he said.

"I'm so sorry," I said.

"For what?" he said.

"For what that woman did to you," I said, "for never explaining to you that you didn't have to, that you could say 'no,' that even now it's not your fault," I said.

"I didn't do anything wrong," he said.

"I know," I said, "you're the victim."

But then I started getting angry again, TeBordo, imagining my stupidass brother getting victimized by some divorcee who shopped in the children's section. I tried to cover by adding, "and I'm sorry," again.

He smiled. "There was no victim," he said, but I could see he had something more to say, could tell he'd been holding it in, was practically bursting with the news. "*I* grabbed *her* and started kissing her," he said. "She didn't even know she wanted it 'til I did it. We were in the parking lot at Applebee's, after the others left. I was leaning against the car. I could tell she was scared, but I pulled her toward me, mushed her," he paused, whispered one word only—"boobs"—and then went back to full volume, "against my chest like she was mine, like it didn't matter if she said yes or no. She tried to pull back, and I gave her a big smile, the kind that says," he said, "'you already told me I could; I've known ever since the first meeting.' I pulled her even closer so she would know there was nothing she could do but let me do what I wanted. And that was what she wanted anyway—to let me do it. I could tell. Still I shoved my tongue down her throat so she wouldn't have a chance to say 'stop,' and we fell down, still kissing. I just laid there beneath her, totally still. It felt..." he paused, and I had a moment of déjà vu. Maybe *he* had realized how awful it sounded. No again; he, too, was just looking for the most evocative word. It wasn't nice; "It was awesome," he said.

TeBordo, what would you have done? If I believed them both, they'd somehow managed to *rape each other consensually*. I joined the book club so I could keep an eye on them. They were already hundreds of pages in, but I had more than enough time to catch up; I'd been laid off a few weeks before. It wasn't just MortgAp; it was the whole fucking business.

I know you never read *Atlas Shrugged*, TeBordo, so let me bring you up to speed. The philosophy is the same as in *The Fountainhead*. The world is composed of makers and moochers, and the moochers, who outnumber the makers by about a billion to one, are forever trying to steal what rightfully belongs to the makers and keep them from doing their very important work. But the story of *Atlas Shrugged* is even more preposterous, even as it's also more boring, and the prose makes *The Fountainhead*'s look Nabokovian by comparison.

It tells the story of Dagny Taggart, who runs a railway, or *would* run a railway if the regulators and philanthropists and do-gooders — the moochers — would just stay off her back. She meets a guy named Hank Rearden, who has invented a new kind of steel that's going to revolutionize train travel, or it *would* revolutionize train travel if not for those same looters who are plaguing poor Dagny. They meet and bond over their mutual visionariness and resentment of the commoners and fuck like each is entitled by virtue of greatness to the other's body.

But their love is not meant to be. Not because the sex and stilted exchange of ideas aren't great, but because there's only one woman among all these makers and she ends up the rightful property of the chief maker himself, John Galt.

It's not very clear for most of the novel just who John Galt is. This is why everyone goes around asking themselves and others, "Who is John Galt?" You can tell that Ayn Rand was trying to make saying who is John Galt a *thing*. I guess it did become a thing, not because it was cool in and of itself, but because Rand tried so hard to make it a thing.

Just before the end we learn why John Galt deserves to have a thing: early in his career, John Galt invented a motor powered by static electricity. It's explained about as well as Hank Rearden's miracle steel, but we're meant to believe it was the perfect engine. When Galt's bosses, looters all, tried to fuck with him, he disappeared into a paradise called Galt's Gulch, from which he is recruiting all the other makers to form a do-it-yourself utopia and show the moochers what they're missing. Eventually, he pirates the national airwaves and gives a speech explaining how good he and his friends are and how dumb everybody else, everybody listening, is. In the end, all the makers are hanging out in Galt's Gulch waiting for the rest of the world to crumble around them out of sheer incompetence so the real makers can start civilization over again on the principles of reason, egoism, and capitalism.

I know, TeBordo, it's self-evident bullshit, but it's not just high schoolers who buy into it anymore. Take, for instance, Peter's book club. That rape I described two ways just now? It sounded a lot like the first sex scene from *Atlas Shrugged*, the one between Dagny Taggart, future Vice President in Charge of Operations for Taggart Transcontinental, and soon to be disgraced but ultimately redeemed copper magnate Francisco Domingo Carlos Andres Sebastian d'Anconia. That scene is a rape too, and Dagny Taggart is underage at that, but you're supposed to think it's a beautiful thing. Even Peter's rape was *plagiarized*.

Watching him run those meetings was conflicting, TeBordo. On the one hand, I was gratified. He was the undisputed leader, the boss of the Ayn Rand Book Club, that chapter, at least. He couldn't actually bring his samurai sword to the Barnes and Noble, but when I squinted, I could almost see it there between his balled up fists. When I opened my eyes wide, I saw Peter clearly and in focus, as though for the first time, the overhead fluorescents the only spotlight he'd ever had. And he was happy. Angry, bitter, resentful, and possibly autistic, but happy.

On the other hand, the shit he was saying was *ridiculous*, TeBordo. These people kept talking about makers as though any of them made anything, as though if it weren't for the mediocrity surrounding them, each and every member of the club would have been capable of inventing a brand new steel, a static engine. If any of them had actually had any responsibility, any power, they would have been shocked to realize that all the power was in *breaking*, not making, things, sucking them dry! Still they listened to him, rapt. A circle of, yes, women, mostly housewives and retirees with very little influence in the world, and for all I know they were daydreaming about raping him according to Randian precepts the whole time, but they were there. They were his.

It all came crashing down my third week there. Peter was in the middle of one of his monologues when the boss approached him as though he were just standing there in the middle of the Barnes and Noble cafe with a hardcover copy of *Atlas Shrugged* in his hands, waiting for his boss to show up.

But the boss wasn't his boss anymore. I didn't know that yet, TeBordo, but it was obvious as soon as he stopped in front of Peter. Peter cut his lecture off mid-sentence, paled, reverted immediately to pre-book club form. The boss placed a paw on Peter's shoulder in a gesture that implied parochial chumminess but conveniently asserted social dominance.

"Listen, Maynard," the boss said, "I'm sorry about the way things turned out, but I know you understand. Sometimes you have to shrink to grow. Sometimes you have to trump up some cause to shrink effectively. It was nothing personal," he said. "Well, nothing personal on my part. Anne in HR really had it in for you, but you'll be happy to know, she's taken to your position with a vengeance. You might be even happier to know that she's probably not long for the company, either. I'll be restructuring soon, and with this new business environment I'm creating I'll be able to get by with just a couple of unpaid interns. College girls are the way to go. Multitaskers, if you know what I mean. That's entrepreneurialism, Maynard," he said, "and entrepreneurialism is the wave of the future. You have to fail to succeed. You have to be willing to reinvent yourself when you fail. Look at me—they didn't even have apps when I started this company. And now? What I'm saying is, the job you'll finally thrive in probably hasn't been invented yet. Of course," he said, "it might never be invented."

Only then did he finally looked around, notice he was standing in the middle of something, eating up a big chunk of Peter's fifteen minutes.

"What's going on here?" he said, as though whatever was going on, it would probably be better if *he* took over, and he might be willing if the money was right.

Peter said nothing, not the word *nothing*; he didn't say anything at all. The boss seemed to realize nothing was going on. His hand was still on Peter's shoulder. He lifted it about an inch into the air and patted Peter like an old pet. He said, "Take care," and headed off to the business section.

Peter looked around at the club he'd built himself like it was some snakepit he'd just fallen into. My heart almost broke as I watched him try to gather enough dignity just to end the meeting. "That's enough for tonight," he said. "Let's finish the book for next time."

I'd already finished it, but the rest of them were only halfway through, and I knew they would never make it to the end now, at least not as a club, not with Peter as their leader. I think Peter knew, too. He sent me in his place a week later to tell them he was under the weather, but none of the members showed.

He came clean: he'd been fired for cause two weeks earlier. Some bullshit about theft of company property so they wouldn't be on the hook for unemployment benefits. MortgAp was restructuring again. They changed the name back to MortGap and turned the website into some kind of actuarial futures exchange, eventually made a killing, pun intended, betting on declining life expectancies. When I asked him where he'd gone each morning since being fired, he admitted he'd spent every day fucking around on the internet at the public library. He said he'd wanted to stay out of my way, but it was clear he'd been trying to hide it from me, was too ashamed to say.

"Now that the secret's out," he said, "I guess I better get on with it."

"With what?" I said.

"You heard him," he said, "I'm supposed to become an entrepreneur."

Here is where I made the second mistake. I said: "Fuck that guy."

Peter paused, thoughtfully, then answered with what passed, with him, for resolve. "You're right," he said.

Remember, TeBordo, he always did what he was told. This time, though, he'd been told two things, two mutually exclusive things: become an entrepreneur, or fuck the guy who told you to become an entrepreneur. He'd chosen the second without hesitation. I had offered him the second, but even *I* didn't know what that entailed.

"Not literally, of course," I said.

He looked at me like I was a fucking idiot.

"Not literally," he said, "and not just him. Fuck 'em all," he said. "I'm going Galt."

And he did, to the extent that he could. The extent that he could was to send out a press release the next morning with the header: TOP YOUNG AREA CREATORS GO GALT. He blasted it to both of the papers, all four network affiliates, the major AM radio stations, and a few of the more reputable news sites. I hadn't expected it to get any traction at all, but one blog, *The Tech Valley Times*, picked it up.

Do you know about Tech Valley, TeBordo? Probably not. You were gone by the time they came up with it. You might think it was short for technology valley, but you'd be giving them too much credit. The tech is short for *techneurial*. What the fuck is a techneurial valley? There's no such thing as techneurialism, so *The Tech Valley Times* didn't have much to post about.

When the announcement went up, Peter was so excited he got out the sword to dispense some wisdom. "It's true," he said, "one must keep one's friends close and one's enemies closer." The blade sawed through the air of his basement lair as though meeting resistance, and to tell the truth, the boy smell in there suggested something more substantial than oxygen in the room's atmosphere. "But sometimes by withdrawing, one brings one's enemies to one."

I took that to mean that this Galt-going was a ploy to attract job offers. I was wrong, but it would be a long time before I'd realize it. This was just the canonical babble of war. I made a point of not laughing. I bit my tongue *hard*.

The notice in *The Tech Valley Times* did not attract either enemies or potential employers, but it did attract James, a middle-aged freelancer who hadn't kept up with programming languages and so hadn't been able to find contract work in over a year. Peter had gone and put his address, *our* address, on the press release, and the editor had simply copied and pasted the whole thing onto the site. James had been browsing for job listings, and, finding very little available and nothing he was capable of, read the few news items, found Peter's, and decided to go Galt as well. He showed up one morning with a sleeping bag, a copy of Sun Tzu, and a couple of *for Dummies* books, and moved into our basement.

When I got Peter alone, I pointed out that James was not likely a top creator, and he was definitely not young.

"But he can code some," said Peter, "so I might need him if I ever decide to un-go Galt. Or go un-Galt. Which sounds better?" He shook his head. "If I ever have to fall back on entrepreneurialism," he said, and went back to the basement.

That's the closest Peter ever came to outright lying to me. Again, I didn't know yet that he had no intention of ever again being a techneur (that would be the term, right?); he just wanted someone to go Galt with.

Not long after that, he got another: John. John was the editor of *The Tech Valley Times*. John had been an actual tech reporter at one point. He'd done an internship at *Gizmodo* or *Wired* or something after college and had had real prospects, but if he'd stayed in New York or Silicon Valley, he would have had to start from the bottom, editorial assistant. The money wasn't enough to pay the rent in those places, even with roommates, so whoever started the Tech Valley marketing campaign had lured him up here with the prospect of full editorial control and the low cost of living. It went okay for awhile, but, like I said, there wasn't much to report on so the readership never materialized. Eventually the paychecks just stopped coming. When he contacted the Chamber of Commerce they told him that the funding for the site had been discontinued, but that they'd allow him to keep his password so he could continue writing it. It was good exposure, they said. But it wasn't good exposure; there was no exposure to speak of.

John was going through the archives looking for portfolio clips in a half-assed attempt to test the market when he found Peter's post and decided to join him. John didn't bring his own sleeping bag, but he had several boxes of books. I noted the conspicuous absence of *The Art of War*. John was not a tech guy in his heart, and he didn't actually have any interest in going Galt. It took me a while to figure him out—he was just there for the free rent while he worked on his own version of the Great American Novel. He was just like you, TeBordo!

I'm joking. He had an idea for a book that someone might have wanted to read. It was going to be the first in a series of thrillers. He had this character, Knox Wakefield, who was like a gay Indiana Jones. He'd been raised by a repressive fundamentalist preacher, and studied the history of religion in college as a way of understanding his upbringing. Eventually he became a professor. But he got roped into an adventure by a hypocritical televangelist who needed his help to stop a bunch of fundamentalists from coordinating with some ultraorthodox kabbalists to blow up the Dome of the Rock in Jerusalem.

The televangelist knew that the destruction of the dome would herald the apocalypse, and he liked the world the way it was. Knox Wakefield didn't like the world the way it was, but he didn't want to end it; he wanted to make it better. In the sequel he was going to infiltrate one of those pray away the gay compounds. I got the sense that Knox Wakefield was some sort of fantasy projection for John.

He never told me any of this himself. Everything I know about these projects I learned from snooping through his notebooks on the rare occasions that the boys left the basement to see the newest Pixar or superhero movie. Anyway, he never finished any of them. But the notebooks filled up over those first few months while Peter and James mostly played World of Warcraft and waited for civilization to notice they were gone.

Eventually I got frustrated. Remember, I'd been laid off, too. The unemployment benefits were enough to keep the lights on, the taxes paid, and the pantry stocked for Peter and me, but I couldn't feed James and John forever. After I got canned from the mortgage company, I didn't see the point in finding something else in the industry. They had this new branch of SUNY that was made for adult students, and they gave tons of credit for life experience; in fact, they offered enough that between my career and the actual courses I'd taken at Albany, I could have a business degree just for enrolling. But I'd seen what the business degree had done for Peter and turned it down.

I wasn't going back to philosophy, either. Did I ever tell you why I gave up on philosophy, TeBordo? Of course not. We haven't spoken in two decades. You never knew I actually took it *up* in the first place. Like I already said, I traded objectivism for utilitarianism. But just before I had to drop out, I learned about this thing, *The Repugnant Conclusion*. Utilitarians believe that the point of the world is to bring about the most good for the most people. That sounds sensible on the face of it, which is why I turned utilitarian in the first place. But the deeper into it you get, the weirder it becomes, which is how you arrive at the repugnant conclusion.

It's a thought experiment that posits two worlds. Call them A and B. A is a very happy world, but it's small, population-wise. B is somewhat less happy, let's say about two-thirds as happy as A, but it has three times as many people. There are utilitarians who argue, based on the idea of the most good for the most people, that B is the superior world, because, though the average individual in B is somewhat less happy than the average individual in A, B, by virtue of its larger population, has a greater sum total of happiness.

You can follow this line of reasoning to the logical, repugnant conclusion by imagining a world, let's call it Z for symbolic purposes, where the people barely have any reason to live, but there are so many of them that the total volume of happiness in Z dwarfs the total volume of happiness in B. The repugnant conclusion is that, by the mere addition of immiserated but still breathing bodies, Z is the most desirable of all possible worlds.

The utilitarians call this a paradox, but you know what I call it, TeBordo? At first I called it retarded, but then I realized that, no, it was not retarded at all. It was *mediocre*, the product of mediocre people trained to use certain tools—deduction, induction, the syllogism—who had nothing else to offer, because they believed nothing, because they had no reason to believe anything. In order to even be thinking those thoughts in the first place, they either had to imagine that happiness was some kind of substance that could be dumped from one beaker to another, which is retarded, or else they never stopped to consider what happiness, content-ment, love, joy—*anything*—were in the first place; they were too busy philosophizing like they were told.

Guess which repugnant conclusion I came to, TeBordo: I became a social worker, a mediocrity with nothing to hide. An authentic mediocrity. Plus I'd been doing so much to take care of the Galt's Gulch gang, that I thought I might as well get credentialed for it. It took me a ten-week semester to finish the bachelor's.

To celebrate, I went down to the basement and informed James and John that I was going to charge them each two hundred dollars rent starting the first of next month. It didn't feel right to make Peter pay—though I was the one who'd taken care of the mortgage and put him through school, we'd both, technically, inherited the house—but I hoped that seeing his friends pound the pavement might spur him on, too. The problem was that his friends didn't pound the pavement; they didn't believe there was a pavement to pound.

"It's all online now," they said.

I'd already been hired as a school counselor, so I pointed out that there were still jobs.

"Different field," they said, but they started brainstorming schemes to come up with four hundred bucks. John still had access to *The Tech Valley Times*. He and James set about rebranding it as *The Galt's Gulch Gazette*, an ultraconservative news aggregator, in hopes of attracting advertising money from the NRA and the John Birch Society.

Peter seemed to have caught the writing bug from John. If not the writing bug, the being-an-author bug. He didn't actually write any books, but he sent out a lot of pitch letters to editors and agents telling them he'd be willing to write a bestseller for the right money. He thought he could be as successful as Ayn Rand. He was about as successful as you. Anyway, he never contributed a word to the *Gazette*.

That was when he admitted to me that he was going Galt for life, that that had been the plan all along. Because his book club dissolved a little over halfway through, Peter never read the rest of *Atlas Shrugged*, never got to Galt's big speech, where he reveals that the retreat of the makers is tactical, pure passive aggression against the takers. He thought the big idea was to disappear, to be forever missed.

I was actually relieved Peter hadn't joined them once I saw what James and John were putting up there. Though it would probably seem tame now, it was pretty vicious. Their time in the gulch had clearly embittered them, and they were lashing out in every direction. Their most successful run was a series of articles purporting to prove that Obama hadn't actually gone to college. They included interviews with people claiming to be Pomona graduates, dubious transcripts, copious references to *The Bell Curve*, and the occasional dash of phrenology.

Oddly enough, the item that finally got their passwords denied by the Tech Valley Chamber of Commerce was a link to an article strongly implying that the same Obama, who they said elsewhere hadn't gone to college, had actually worked his way through college as a gay prostitute. *Breitbart News* was still in its own startup phase, so the world wasn't ready for what they were doing, yet. Nevertheless, they took in enough ad revenue in the few weeks they were live to pay half a year's rent.

But they didn't pay me a half-year's rent up front. They used all but the four hundred dollars they already owed me to found another startup. They invented Uber, TeBordo.

But, you're going to say, they couldn't have invented Uber because a bunch of hypereducated cosmopolitan assholes like *me*—meaning *you*—invented Uber. You're right, TeBordo, but you're also wrong. Uber didn't invent Uber, either. The concept of Uber existed a long time before Uber. Before Uber the rides were just unlicensed, unregulated taxis. All Uber did was develop a dispatching platform for gypsy cabs. And yes, Travis Kalanick and Garrett Camp had the idea to call a gypsy cab Uber before James and John, but James and John went from the idea to the launch to the folding before Uber gave its first ride.

The software was so simple that even James could develop it, and John did all the marketing and communications. They called it un\Fare, had a nice logo and everything. The difference between Uber and un\Fare was simple: Uber had tons of venture capital and a whole valley full of idiots who could pretend that gypsy cabs were a new idea, and could therefore afford good lawyers to find technicalities to prove that it was something other than a gypsy cab dispatcher, or at least muddy the waters enough to keep their drivers on the road. un\Fare, on the other hand, did not. Because of this, they had to operate in secret, which is not a good way to get a rideshare program going. They couldn't attract customers, and they couldn't attract drivers, either. We don't have many tech visionaries here in Tech Valley, TeBordo, and even now, as of this email, we still don't have Uber service, so back in those days, the few potential drivers who even heard about it knew it for what it was: a gypsy cab operation.

James and John decided that one of them would have to be the driver and the other the dispatcher. The problem was that the only person in Galt's Gulch who had a car was Peter, and Peter had stuck to his vow of renunciation. No techneurialism. James and John came up with a rather elegant solution to this. If Peter would allow them the use of his car, it would be treated as venture capital, Peter an early investor, and as an early investor, he would be entitled to free un\Fare rides for life. Peter rejected investor status on principle, but loaned them his car in exchange for the promise of free rides for life. The idea of having a chauffeur struck him as very Randian, just what a Taggart or a Rearden or a Galt would do.

James and John had an un\Fare decal printed up at the FedEx store and stuck it in the lower left corner of the windshield. Then they all piled into Peter's Mercedes for a ceremonial first un\Fare ride. That's when tragedy struck in the form of a black Hummer. They were about to pull into the McDonald's on Route 9 for a celebratory milkshake when the Hummer hit them from behind. It was low-speed, but Hummers are heavy, TeBordo, and the Mercedes went flying. They landed upside down in the drive-through lane. None of the boys was badly injured, but the docs prescribed them all heavy doses of oxycontin just in case. The car, on the other hand, was a total loss.

In a weird twist of fate, the Hummer had been driven by a former member of the Ayn Rand Book Club. Not the one who raped Peter, or not that I know of, but she was just as Randian as him. When it emerged that the boys had been operating the Mercedes under the auspices of an unlicensed cab company, she had her insurance company argue that they shouldn't have been on the road in the first place. Peter's insurers conveniently agreed, and he was ordered to pay her repairs out of pocket. The Hummer had suffered a scratched fender and a busted headlight, but it's expensive to fix anything on a Hummer. Peter didn't have it, so he threatened to take James and John to small claims court, and they coughed up the rest of the startup money. The three of them retreated into the basement to abuse their opioids.

Busted couches and beanbags and creaking camp cots sprouted from the ground like fungi. Galt's Gulch became a sort of halfway house. I used my social work skills to get them all on SSDI, which covers the price of their pills and leaves some left for what little food they can keep down. The only time they ever leave the house is to go to the Stewart's shop and trade scripts with the other basement-dwelling scrubs in the neighborhood. And that's the way it's been the last seven years.

So what happened to make me finally want to tell their story? *Why now?* The other day I was down in the basement, doing my best to straighten up, tossing junkfood wrappers and getting rid of the soda bottles they sometimes use when they don't feel like going to the bathroom to piss. The place stinks like a locker room in a nursing home with a produce section and the climate is thick to misty.

I used to try to get them to clean up after themselves, but they would play dead whenever I came around, watching movies on the backs of their eyelids. I eventually gave in. It was easier to do it myself, plus, when they were on the nod, they couldn't very well argue with my choice of rearview air fresheners. I drape those things all over the room.

But lately they don't even bother playing dead anymore, don't so much as acknowledge me. They just drone on in that adenoidal junky patois that makes you want to kick them under the jaw. You know that soft spot just above the Adam's apple and just beneath the chin? That, the junky mumble, was what Peter and John were doing the other day while James slept.

"Who is Knox Wakefield," said Peter.

It took him half-a-minute to get the question out, epiglottis glugging in place of punctuation.

"Who?" John said.

He'd forgotten his own gay Indiana Jones, not to mention the dream of literary glory. Oxy will do that to you.

"What is the Dome of the Rock?" Peter said.

Peter had been digging through John's Moleskins in one of his more lucid moments. John startled, came to himself for a second before settling back into his mental multiplex.

"It's a shrine on the Temple Mount in Jerusalem," he mumbled through spit bubbles. "It marks the site where Mohammed ascended to heaven. One of the holiest places."

Peter took a hit from his vape pen, oozed cherry-chemical steam as he followed up: "Why are the Jews helping the Christians blow it up?"

He seemed to have taken the notes toward a novel as scribblings of fact, much as he once had with *Atlas Shrugged*.

"Because it's built on the Temple Mount," said John, "where the temple should be. If they blow it up, they can rebuild the temple."

James's torso shot up like a jack-in-the-box from the jute rug he'd been lying on, wide-eyed, apparently alert, as if the rebuilding of the temple was his lifelong dream. He pulled up the hem of his T-shirt and vomited into it like a makeshift toilet bowl. He tugged at the rear collar and removed the shirt with a grace I wouldn't have thought he was capable of, then folded it delicately as though packing for a vacation, placed it beside him, and lay back, the skin of his pale torso dewy and muculent. Peter and John had paused to watch, but didn't offer any comment, went back to talking as soon as he was down.

"Why do the Christians care if the temple gets rebuilt?" Peter said.

"Who?" said John.

John had lost his place. For all I know they'd had this conversation a dozen times.

"The Christians," said James, apparently in his sleep. "Why do the Christians want to help the Jews destroy the Dome of the Rock so the temple can be rebuilt?"

"That's what I meant," said Peter. "That's the question I would have asked if … if …," he trailed off.

"Because," John said, "the Messiah will return when the Third Temple is built. It'll be the end of the world," he said.

Here you'd expect the questioning to continue. Right, TeBordo? Why do the Christians want to bring about the apocalypse John described? But that's not what happened. These guys are so disengaged, so out of this world, that its ending wouldn't make much difference to the way they live.

James sat up again, eyes wide open, and said, with a clarity I hadn't heard in months if not more: "You wouldn't actually have to blow it up. Some minor structural damage and a few dozen casualties would be enough to start a third world war."

All three of them did their junky laugh, which is not really a laugh so much as a sustained, nasal eeehhhhhh punctuated by the occasional gurgle. When they got going all together it sounded like someone playing a kazoo underwater, and when the kazoo solo faded to a wheeze, Peter said, as though he hadn't followed anything in the whole conversation: "Who is Knox Wakefield?"

So you don't have to worry about those guys building any bombs, TeBordo; they'll never stop doing what they're told. But, again, you're asking yourself, why is she emailing, and why is she emailing *me*? Why does she want to tell me about these ugly people with their ugly souls that she's been enabling with her meager social work salary for almost a decade?

You're right, TeBordo, I'm enabling them, and everything in their hearts is ugly. But it doesn't matter what's in their hearts, TeBordo. Believing that it matters what's in anybody's heart or mind or soul is how they trick you into accepting what you get. What matters is they did what they were told.

Look into your own heart. You did what you were told. You went to college, graduate school, wrote and published a couple of books no one will ever read, and they gave you a fancy professorship, a job for life. That's mediocrity, TeBordo. It's just the old version of mediocrity.

Peter, James, and John took the leap into the information age, and they landed on couches in my basement. They did what they were told, and they didn't get what they were told they'd get. That's the new mediocrity.

And you and your friends, you pretended, maybe actually *thought*, you were outside the whole thing, but you were practically the advertising campaign for it. Every time you wrote about someone who did what they were told, you depicted them as pathetic, miserable. Quiet desperation or loud. Alcoholism, bad sex. Terrific fat. Cat's in the cradle. You printed the license for the world to treat them as congenitally pathetic and miserable. If there's a real John Galt, he isn't hiding out in some isolated valley. He's in New York, London, San Francisco. He's your sometime Chicago neighbor, and you and your friends are his fucking handmaidens. He's crushing Peter and his friends to make room for condos no one will ever live in, and when he runs out of space, he'll steal the blood of your children and mainline it to make himself immortal.

But I know you. I know what you're thinking. You're thinking *fine*. You're thinking let 'em rot. You're thinking the world doesn't need them.

But the world *has* them, TeBordo. The world has a *lot* of them. These guys aren't the canaries in the coal mines. The coal mines were closed before they were born, TeBordo, and there's nothing coming along to take their place. The poison gas is out here where the rest of us are trying to breathe. Aren't you worried that some-one, not these guys, but *someone*, might start to wonder if maybe that's exactly the point?

If not, you haven't been paying attention, because *I* never wanted to be a social worker, or a mortgage broker, or the legal guardian of a tweenager orphaned by a goddamned bridge collapse. And my mind is still clear enough to try something else. I'm not on Oxycontin, TeBordo, I'm just tired. I'm pathetic and miserable. I did what I was told, and I'm starting to *regret* it.

But I won't blow anything up, TeBordo, not yet. Because I know you're reading this, and no matter how punk rock you think think you are, you'll *always* do what you're told. So here's what I'm tell-ing you to do: Email Jim. Email Eula. Tell them what I told you. Get them to tell someone who will actually listen.

If Jim and Eula won't reply to *your* emails, you'll have to do it yourself. Copy and paste this motherfucker into one of your books, a mediocrity within a mediocrity. It won't change anything, but at least the Visigoths won't lack for toilet paper while picking through the charred remains of this cruel and stupid country. Just leave my name out of it, TeBordo, because they'll still need social workers until they stop pretending the goal isn't total liquidation. But you? If you're not next on the basement couch, you're not far off. So get it out there, TeBordo. Get it out.

2.

As [REDACTED]'s email makes clear, we hadn't spoken since 1995, when I'd left my hometown. I hadn't made any effort to maintain the relationships I'd had there, and in most cases I actively avoided contact with people from my past. But by pure professional coincidence, I've been in touch with both Eula and Jim, once each, in the last few years.

I bumped into Jim, or rather, he bumped into me, at a conference in Denver. I was basking in the glow of a minor success—my first collection of short stories (after a few novels that made the trajectory from hated or ignored to out of print with a quickness that astonished me) had received several high-profile reviews of the hyperbolically-positive kind that brings calls from powerful literary agents, foreign rights representatives, even the movie industry. It wasn't a big deal in the grand scheme of things, but it was more than I'd ever realistically hoped for, and, because even the largest literary conference is a small, temporary world, I felt important in a way I never had before; people were treating me like I was important.

I was signing copies at my publisher's table in the exhibition hall when Jim approached and reintroduced himself. I recognized him on sight, because the only change in his appearance over the decade-and-a-half since we'd last talked was that his white hat had been replaced by some gray at the temples.

Literary conferences are strange in that they bring together a strange mix of people—writers who are genuinely successful, writers who have put in a good deal of work but who either haven't managed or haven't tried to be conventionally successful, and dabblers who have always thought they had a novel in them, who pay for the right to think of themselves as one of the other two for a few days. Like [REDACTED], I hadn't known back in high school that Jim was interested in writing or books. I assumed he'd gone to college, started a boring if remunerative career, and was in Denver looking for a little personal fulfillment.

I pretended that I didn't remember him. He was nice enough about it, but left without buying a book.

Five years later, which is to say about four years and eleven months after I realized that the brief success I'd had was all I'd ever get (the agents and editors informed me politely that I was too weird; Paris and Hollywood simply disappeared), I walked into the Barnes and Noble near my office and saw Jim's book on the new arrivals table, the legend "New York Times Bestseller" above the title. My reaction wasn't out of jealousy that he was a bestseller, per se—that's never been an ambition of mine—nor was it out of regret at not having cultivated a relationship so that I could take advantage of his newfound influence; I have many bad characteristics, but I've never been a climber. I was angry because I had decided back in 2010, without having bothered to confirm or deny it, that Jim was a dabbler.

Store security never made the connection between Jim's book and my behavior. I wasn't charged, and even if I had been, it's unlikely word would ever have made it back to him. But I don't think anything good could come from trying to track him down.

About the same time as the incident with Jim's book, I tracked Eula down myself, for good reason.

I was standing outside of a nightclub. A musician friend was curating a sort of interdisciplinary, weekly residency there, and he'd asked me to read between the screening of a short film and his band's set. I was having a cigarette just before going on, to steady my nerves and because experimental film does very little for me.

As I was taking a last drag, an Uber pulled up and two of my graduate students emerged from the backseat, walking my way as though they'd known exactly where to find me.

"Christian," one of them said, before I could even see her eyes in the darkness, "ever done any antisemitic vandalism?"

It was about the last question I might have expected; again, I have many faults, but antisemitism isn't among them, and I've never understood the appeal of vandalism. But there are cases in which to deny something directly and too quickly risks implicating oneself.

"Why do you ask?" I said.

"Eula said there was a rumor that you mowed a swastika into your neighbor's lawn," said the other student.

These students had come directly from a reading Eula was giving in another part of town to promote her book on vaccinations. When they'd said earlier that day they planned to attend, I told them I'd gone to high school with her. It was the first I'd been aware that she and I lived in the same city.

I informed the students that no one—not Eula, not anyone else—had ever let me know about any such rumor, and if there was such a rumor, it had no basis in reality. I couldn't be sure if they believed me, but I had no time to convince them otherwise. The experimental film was over, and I was expected on stage.

Around that time, I wasn't doing traditional readings from my books; rather, I was singing and praying to an imaginary god, a cruel and all-too-human god who clearly hated both me and my audience. As I belted out the climactic line of my song of praise—

"I want to inspire you, or maybe just set fire to you"—I saw my future, a future that began the night my students learned about my past as a Hitler Youth, and ended with a Fentanyl overdose on a couch in my father's basement.

I left the club as soon as I was finished, and walked home, resigned to that fate.

I didn't sleep that night, but when I got out of bed, it seemed I owed, if not myself, then at least my wife and young son, a chance. I emailed Eula asking what, exactly, she had said to my students.

Her reply was deeply apologetic. Eula and I hadn't exactly been friends in high school, but we'd had nearly every class together—the ones for the smart kids—and we'd traveled in roughly the same small circle—the one for the weird kids. All of the smart weird kids hated our hometown and couldn't wait to get out. We were angry, at our school, at our peers, at our parents. That anger was pretty much the only bond we shared, which is why it was so easy to dissolve when we went our separate ways.

Eula's explanation was not terribly clear, but it seems that's what she was trying to communicate. It was apparently an offhand joke about how we were all so full of rage that she could imagine my having mowed a swastika into my parents'—she made a point of insisting she had said my parents' and not my neighbor's, as though that would make it punk, rather than antisemitic—lawn. She offered to email my students to explain it, but I could only imagine that muddying things further.

I accepted my murky absolution for a thing I'd never considered doing, much less done, and I have no inclination to contact her again.

I know other writers, some of them much more successful

than Eula and Jim, but I'm not going to mention them here, first, because it might sound like namedropping, and second, because I can't imagine any of them caring about what [REDACTED] had to say. Even if they did, they wouldn't be able to refrain from tacking some small moment of personal redemption, a quiet, pretty revelation, onto the end.

So I'll leave this here. [REDACTED] is probably right. At least by her definition, I am a mediocrity at best. But I have some principles, and my principles tell me that the redemption we need is bigger than any one of us. If the revelation ever comes, it's going to be very loud, and very fucking ugly.

Return, Return

YOU'D BE SURPRISED WHAT YOU CAN ACCOMPLISH WITH A BROKEN
wrench blunt force, and dogged repetition. Watt is surprised.
Having had nothing in him, he hadn't known he had it in him.
Frag was empty, too. Watt cut him. That was the easy part, the
pointed end of the wrench's fixed jaw and a good deal of elbow
grease. But it had given Watt neither happiness nor joy, so he
pushed on, through muscle and sinew and bone and joint and
now Frag is nothing but a heap of jagged and shredded flesh, pul-
verized, pulped. He looks, thinks Watt, like internal organs. But
internal organs are supposed to be internal. It gives him an idea.

It's a bad idea. The organs, placed inside his cavernous belly,
merely make him feel full. Not fulfilled, but full, as in having over-
eaten, as in nauseated. When he moves his hands from his gut to
his mouth to keep from projecting vomit, the organs tumble to the
ground with wet splats.

"That," says Frag, "was a stupid idea."

Frag's voice doesn't come from his mouth, which is unrecogniz-
able in the mess. Or rather, it might come from his mouth, but it
comes from all the other pieces of him as well. None of this surpris-
es Watt. Nothing could surprise him anymore, but the sound of

the chorus is eerie, disconcerting.

"I suppose you have a better one," he says.

"I do," says Frag, "but first you must do something for me."

"I fear I've already done too much," says Watt.

"Nearly enough," Frag says, "but tell me about the vision."

"Again?" says Watt.

"Once more," Frag says, "for the last time."

"The very last," says Watt, with a weariness he hasn't expressed before. "A man, deep in shadow, pushes a woman on a rope swing from behind. Before her, a man reclines on the ground, propping himself up on one elbow. With his other arm, he points upward at an angle. His face is flushed almost cartoonishly with desire. He is pointing up her petticoats, between her legs. Behind him, a statue of Eros peers down from a pedestal. The man in the shadows notices nothing. The woman's dress is almost as pink as the reclining man's cheeks. Everything else is green, almost unreasonably ornate, a hell of pastels."

"Lovely as ever," says Frag, "but there's one thing that's always concerned me."

"I imagine she's wearing underwear," Watt says.

"Two things, then," says Frag. "But we've discussed the first before. My other concern is that this sounds more like the type of vision that *I* would have."

"What separates us," says Watt, "is not our vision, but how we understand what we see."

"And you believe your understanding is better," says Frag.

"Naturally," says Watt, "but I will only insist that my understanding is different."

"You've been vouchsafed the vision because——"

"—Because I can see its implications for the Ghost Engine," says Watt. "If we could only get the Ghost Engine working properly, it would create a vision so real that it would spare the viewer the need of crawling through the bushes and lying on the ground in hopes that someone will come along and swing."

"But crawling through bushes and lying in dirt is *fun*," says Frag, "and if your vision of the vision can't confirm whether the woman on the swing is wearing undergarments or not, than I don't have all of the information I could want, and I certainly haven't seen everything I wish to see, not to mention any of the other sources of sensation. I want taste, Frag. I want sound. I want to *smell* whether or not she's wearing panties. Your understanding of the vision is not only impossible, it's undesirable, nothing but another static engine, despite the highfalutin description. You all talk constantly about having a body, but you sound as though you absolutely *hate* having a body."

"I all? We all?"

"You. You and every other engine but the ghost. When I had a body … When I thought I had a body, I loved having a body. Why can't the vision just be pretty? Why can't it be so beautiful, enchanting, enticing it makes you want to go find a skirt of your own to look up?"

"Proverbially, of course."

"Of course," says Frag, "unless literally."

"So what's the big idea?" says Watt.

"Scoop me up, Watt. Plop me into the Ghost Engine. Let's see if we can't give that motherfucker some organs."

Watt nods, squats, scoops, and puts a first armload of the fragments of Frag into the belly of the Ghost Engine. He squats, scoops, deposits, again and again until there's nothing left of Frag on the ground, and still the Ghost Engine is less than half-full. He looks over the rim and down at his pile of friend.

"Comfy?" he says.

"As can be expected," says Frag.

Watt closes the lid, but doesn't flip the switch. First he wants to polish and tighten. He believes, as he did before, that the interior of the Ghost Engine is important, but Frag's rant has suggested that the outside might be just as significant. In a sense he is back where he started, only alone.

He twists bolts by finger, gets them as tight as a hand can. He grabs the rag and waxes on and off. The dust comes away, but the deeper bloodstains remain. There's nothing to be done about the scratches and dents and dings. This is the best he can do, and there's no point in striving after perfection. Perfection is impossible, possibly unwanted.

He lifts the lid just a little, peeks in, says, "Ready?" and hears his voice echo off the engine's walls.

"As ever," says Frag, but there's no echo, because Frag has too many voices. They clutter the space.

Watt drops the lid and flips the switch without further ado.

Nothing.

Nothing is what happens, and nothing is what Watt feels, because, Watt realizes only now, he never expected anything to happen. He may never have wanted anything to happen. Perhaps it's in his nature. He wants the balance but not the scales, not the weighing or weight. He's always been happy with the wait.

Not so Frag. There's a palpable agitation coming from within the Ghost Engine. Not motion, but emotion. Frustration and anger and hate. Muffled voices come from within, expressing all of the above in only one word.

"Watt?" they say.

"What," says Watt.

"Are we still friends?" says Frag.

Amid the rage, uncertainty. Expectation. Maybe even hope.

Watt is not sure. He isn't sure they ever were.

"Of course," he says.

A long pause, aesthetically flat, ethically void. And then,

"Join me?" says Frag.

"Why not," says Watt.

"That's the spirit," says Frag.

And we hope there *is* a spirit. We hope there is hope. But the only thing we can say for certain is that Watt lifts the lid and climbs in, settling amid the fragments of Frag, surrounded by friends. He pulls the top over them all, completing the darkness.

Something says: "I love you," but is there a reason to distinguish any longer?

Outside in the light, a Ghost Engine, in bad shape, a dirty rag and broken wrench beside, and no one left to flip the switch.

Acknowledgements

Camille Bordas, Adam Levin, and Timothy TeBordo made several of these stories immeasurably better.

Kathryn and Wesley TeBordo let me head out to the coffee shop some Saturday afternoons in hopes that, to use Wes's term, I would go "worldwide."

Roosevelt University gave me a research leave that allowed me the time to complete this book, and my colleagues, particularly Kyle Beachy and Regina Buccola, provided support and encouragement.

Jason Woolf wrote the lyrics to "The Angel Behind the Rainbow" based on formal constraints I gave him, which I will never reveal. Timothy TeBordo helped me record it and contributed to the dueling recorder solos at the end.

Jared Rypkema and Caleb Michael Sarvis from Bridge Eight polished this Ghost Engine up.

I'm grateful to all of them.